Mending Hearts in Crystal Cove

A Thief, a Chef and a Second Chance
The sequel to Books, Pens & Larceny

Northport Booksellers Spring Farm NSW Australia 2570

Copyright © 2024 by José F. Nodar

All rights reserved. No part of this publication may be reproduced, distributed, or transmitted in any form or by any means, including photocopying, recording, or other electronic or mechanical methods, without the prior written permission of the publisher, except in the case of brief quotations embodied in critical reviews and certain other non-commercial uses permitted by copyright law. Copyright of this publication is owned by José F. Nodar. The individual authors keep copyright of the individual stories/poetry.

Publisher's Note: This is a work of fiction. Names, characters, places and incidents are a product of the author's imagination. Locales and public names are sometimes used for atmospheric purposes. Any resemblance to actual people, living or dead, or to businesses, companies, events, institutions, or locales is completely coincidental.

Mending Hearts in Crystal Cove/ José F. Nodar. -- 1st ed.
ISBN 978-0-9756281-7-1- Paperback
ISBN 978-0-9756281-8-8- E-book
ISBN 978-0-9756281-9-5 -Audiobook

Dedication

To my wife Miriam, who has supported me in every step of the way. I love you heaps, my muse!

To my daughter and stepdaughters, who have put up with all my mistakes and suffered through all my horrible jokes.

Additionally, I extend my gratitude to my grandchildren and step-grandchild for enduring my quirks and eccentricities throughout the years.

And I special thank you to my friends who have patiently listened to my endless chatter about my writing endeavours.

To my fellow partners in crime, authors in the family of Camden Books and Quick Story Tales who have supported me in so many ways. I am forever grateful for your trust and friendship.

Could not have done with without the help of my copyeditor/proofreader, book cover designer and my audiobook narrators. Thank you for making me look good!

Finally, my heartfelt thanks to the wonderful readers that have purchased my books in the past and I hope will continue to do so in the future.

It's all for you.

Mending Hearts In Crystal Cove

Chapter One – No Longer Certain..6
Chapter Two – Grand Opening 13
Chapter Three – Crystal Cove 16
Chapter Four – The Best..22
Chapter Five - Barby..28
Chapter Six – The Poplar Inn 32
Chapter Seven – The Seashell Café...38
Chapter Eight – Shore Drive 44
Chapter Nine – Antonia 'Toni' Webster...49
Chapter Ten – Interesting Dinner 51
Chapter Eleven – Making Friends 57
Chapter Twelve – Ride Home 63
Chapter Thirteen – The Captain and the First Mate 69
Chapter Fourteen – Home Whitham...76
Chapter Fifteen – Lititz Carter..84
Chapter Sixteen – The Cloud Nine Express Trail..91
Chapter Seventeen – An Aroma and a Petal..97
Chapter Eighteen – Opening Up to Toni...99
Chapter Nineteen – A Better Time...105
Chapter Twenty – New Hope 114
Chapter Twenty - One - Surprise..116
Chapter Twenty-Two – Echoes of Love 123
Chapter Twenty - Three - Magia..127
Chapter Twenty - Four - Diet...130
Chapter Twenty-Five - Suspicious 136
Chapter Twenty-Six – A Good Place..141
Chapter Twenty-Seven – Wild Rumours 147
Chapter Twenty-Eight - Reactions 153
Chapter Twenty-Nine – There is Always Tomorrow 159
Chapter Thirty – Mi Media Naranja...163
Chapter Thirty-One – A Sneaky One 166
Chapter Thirty-Two – Albert and His Timing...173
Chapter Thirty-Three – Conclusions 178
Chapter Thirty-Four - Bait..184
Chapter Thirty-Five – Going Shopping...187
Chapter Thirty-Six – Not a Bad Idea 191

Dedication

To my wife Miriam, who has supported me in every step of the way. I love you heaps, my muse!

To my daughter and stepdaughters, who have put up with all my mistakes and suffered through all my horrible jokes.

Additionally, I extend my gratitude to my grandchildren and step-grandchild for enduring my quirks and eccentricities throughout the years.

And I special thank you to my friends who have patiently listened to my endless chatter about my writing endeavours.

To my fellow partners in crime, authors in the family of Camden Books and Quick Story Tales who have supported me in so many ways. I am forever grateful for your trust and friendship.

Could not have done with without the help of my copyeditor/proofreader, book cover designer and my audiobook narrators. Thank you for making me look good!

Finally, my heartfelt thanks to the wonderful readers that have purchased my books in the past and I hope will continue to do so in the future.

It's all for you.

Mending Hearts In Crystal Cove

Chapter One – No Longer Certain..6
Chapter Two – Grand Opening 13
Chapter Three – Crystal Cove 16
Chapter Four – The Best..22
Chapter Five - Barby...28
Chapter Six – The Poplar Inn 32
Chapter Seven – The Seashell Café..38
Chapter Eight – Shore Drive 44
Chapter Nine – Antonia 'Toni' Webster..49
Chapter Ten – Interesting Dinner 51
Chapter Eleven – Making Friends 57
Chapter Twelve – Ride Home 63
Chapter Thirteen – The Captain and the First Mate 69
Chapter Fourteen – Home Whitham..76
Chapter Fifteen – Lititz Carter...84
Chapter Sixteen – The Cloud Nine Express Trail..91
Chapter Seventeen – An Aroma and a Petal...97
Chapter Eighteen – Opening Up to Toni...99
Chapter Nineteen – A Better Time..105
Chapter Twenty – New Hope 114
Chapter Twenty - One - Surprise...116
Chapter Twenty-Two – Echoes of Love 123
Chapter Twenty - Three - Magia..127
Chapter Twenty - Four - Diet...130
Chapter Twenty-Five - Suspicious 136
Chapter Twenty-Six – A Good Place...141
Chapter Twenty-Seven – Wild Rumours 147
Chapter Twenty-Eight - Reactions 153
Chapter Twenty-Nine – There is Always Tomorrow 159
Chapter Thirty – Mi Media Naranja..163
Chapter Thirty-One – A Sneaky One 166
Chapter Thirty-Two – Albert and His Timing..173
Chapter Thirty-Three - Conclusions 178
Chapter Thirty-Four - Bait..184
Chapter Thirty-Five – Going Shopping..187
Chapter Thirty-Six – Not a Bad Idea 191

Chapter Thirty-Seven – Bawling Like a Baby 196
Chapter Thirty-Eight – The Three Musketeers 202
Chapter Thirty-Nine – Broadway Song 207
Chapter Forty – Irish Coffee 210
Chapter Forty-One – Not a Bad Holiday Trip 215
Chapter Forty-Two - Decision 219
Chapter Forty-Three – What To Do About Danny? 221
Chapter Forty-Four – Action 223
Chapter Forty-Five – All Set 227
Chapter Forty-Six – Special Friendship 231
Chapter Forty-Seven – Captain Cora 237
Chapter Forty-Eight – Second Watch 242
Chapter Forty-Nine – Phone Ping 244
Chapter Fifty – Peter Cooke 250
About the Author 259

Chapter One – No Longer Certain

Sitting alone at his favourite table at the *White Sheep* Danny Monk couldn't shake the feeling that time had slowed to a crawl. He had so many feelings going through his mind. He popped the question seven months ago to Alessia Vassallo and got a surprising response.

"Well..." is what Alessia said, as her voice trailed off, leaving Danny in a state of suspended animation. He felt his heart pounding, and the seconds stretched into eternity. He wanted to fill the silence with words, with laughter, with relief, but he was trapped in this fragile moment, unable to predict which way it would sway.

Danny still remembers that moment as if time were inching forward, and Alessia's lips curled into a small smile, a mixture of happiness and uncertainty. He remembers his heart leaping, but the word 'Well...' still echoed in his mind. The enthusiastic 'Yes!' he had hoped for didn't come. It wasn't the jubilant response that would have unleashed a torrent of emotions, love and celebration. There was something unusual about it, something he couldn't quite categorise. A simple answer: "Well....," that trailed off into an abyss.

At that moment seven months ago, he felt he needed to do something. The tension of the moment was unbearable. He wanted to blur out to her: "Alessia, I meant every word I said. I want to spend the rest of my life with you. But I need to know, what's on your mind? What's behind that *'Well...'*?"

He did not get his answer.

Alessia simply went to the front door, unlocked it and without looking back, left, leaving him and his spiritual partner, Albert Matthew Guzman, in shock.

Seven months later, as Danny takes a sip of his favourite drink, a Mojito, and then he sees his best friend walk into the pub and, as always, Albert is dressed to the nines.

"Danny, honey, I knew you would be here. I drove by the bookstore, saw it was closed and no lights upstairs in your bachelor's pad, so I figure this will be the place you would be, and I was right." Albert gestures to Maire and does the two-finger motions to my drink for her to get Angus the bartender to create and bring two to the table.

"So darling, talk to me. You are not here moping, are you?"

"No, I am not Albert," Danny said with a half-hearted voice.

"Good, because I have a lot to pass on to you on the progress of our new venture, *'Locks & Loaded'* We are ninety-eight per cent ready to open on schedule. I am just waiting for confirmation from Northport Council that the mayor will attend and do the honours of opening the store for business. We have all eight chairs booked all day. It will be a fabulous opening, just marvellous!"

"Oh, I know it will be Albert, I have no doubt. You got some good folks that came with you from *'Cut Me Crazy'*, which pissed off the mob that bought you out, but like you know, they cannot put everything in the sales contract and forgetting the non-compete clause, well that was a fluke, so all was fair."

"Agree Danny sweetness, so glad our attorney saw the avenue was open, and we pounced on it," Albert giggled a bit as he said that.

Marie walks up with the two Mojitos and picks up Danny's empty glass and, with her usual smile, walks back to the bar.

Taking his first sip, Albert lets off a slight sigh. "Lovely, as always. You did not teach Marie how to make these, did you, sweet boy?"

That puts a smile on Danny's face: "No, I did not Albert. It is all her," and he takes his own sip. *"Yes, darn good Mojito,"* Danny thinks to himself.

"You will be at the grand opening, right, Danny?"

"Of course, Albert. It is our day to shine and let Northport know that the best hair salon in all of Sydney is now open for business."

"I will drink to that statement," responds Albert, gulping down his Mojito and motioning to Marie to bring another two drinks.

"Whoa Albert, this will be my fourth one and I have not had lunch."

"Well, that makes two of us with no lunch, so let's order something for I too am getting hungry," responds Albert, reaching for the lunch menus and passing Danny one.

After a brief glance, Albert has his answer: "This sounds good. How about we order two pan-fried abalone with zucchini and garlic? Sounds delicious. Maybe add some garlic bread to soak up the juices and some salad with avocados. Love those darlings."

It did not take Danny long to agree, and he gets up and approaches Marie, who was speaking with Angus, at the bar and places the order and heads to the toilet.

Danny walked into the toilet but not to relive himself. He was a camel, and this moment was no different. He wanted to splash some water on his face. Albert asked if he was moping, and he say no, but he was and needed to snap out of it.

The last seven months have been exciting with the new business startup, but miserable because of Alessia's response to his marriage proposal. He needed to get out of this mental state, just like Albert said.

As Danny stood in front of the mirror, surrounded by the shadows of his own thoughts, he realised he couldn't keep moping around forever. His world had become a monotonous loop of self-pity and doubt, and he knew he had to break free from it. His life had come to a standstill, and he yearned for change, for something different. Two things he knew for sure; first, his 'acquisition days' were over and second, karma has a way of coming back and biting you in the arse so he was not going to take any more chances.

He rubbed his tired eyes and let out a deep sigh. It was time to act, to clear his head and find the peace he so desperately needed. Danny reached for his phone and began scrolling through photos he had taken during happier times. Among them, he stumbled upon a picture of a serene beach up north, with the sun setting over the horizon. That was it. The inspiration he needed.

With newfound determination, Danny set his plan in motion. He returned to the table ready to have his lunch and even tell his dear friend his plan.

"My sweet boy, you were there a long time. No issues?" a smart-arse Albert insinuated.

"No Albert, rather inspiration. I will share after our meal where my mind went to, and here comes Marie with our garlic bread and salad. Let's dig in."

The avocado salad was a simple plate of sliced avocados, a smattering of finely cut onions and small cherry tomatoes sprinkled with a few flecks of parmesan cheese. Strange, but Danny knew that the *'White Sheep'* pub chef was not your ordinary pub cook. *"Just look at the menu selection,"* Danny thought. Who would think a pub would have pan-fried abalone with zucchini and garlic as a lunch special?

The fish arrived before they could finish the garlic bread and it looked just wonderful and the aroma was divine just in itself. Serve in a deep dish, the juices just surrounded the fish fillets, and the poor abalone was quickly devoured.

"Now that was an excellent choice if I do not say so myself, which I did," cracking one of his silly laughs, said Albert.

"Now what was this epiphany you arrived to in the toilet?"

"Let's order a sherry before I start, OK?"

"I never say no to alcohol darling, you know me," as Albert waves to Marie, who came over, took the order for two Harvey Bristol Cream drinks, which does not take her long to deliver.

After taking a sip, Danny starts.

"Albert, I need some time off. Away from *'Village Books & Stuff,'* not here for our new venture *'Locks & Loaded'* I need time to relax and see what I need to do to get over this failure with Alessia."

"I see," said Albert, gulping his sherry down, surprised at Danny's statement. "Where and for how long, my sweet boy, are you thinking of going?"

Danny takes out his phone and shows Albert his inspiration photo.

"Nice. So, you were there before?"

splash some water on his face. Albert asked if he was moping, and he say no, but he was and needed to snap out of it.

The last seven months have been exciting with the new business startup, but miserable because of Alessia's response to his marriage proposal. He needed to get out of this mental state, just like Albert said.

As Danny stood in front of the mirror, surrounded by the shadows of his own thoughts, he realised he couldn't keep moping around forever. His world had become a monotonous loop of self-pity and doubt, and he knew he had to break free from it. His life had come to a standstill, and he yearned for change, for something different. Two things he knew for sure; first, his 'acquisition days' were over and second, karma has a way of coming back and biting you in the arse so he was not going to take any more chances.

He rubbed his tired eyes and let out a deep sigh. It was time to act, to clear his head and find the peace he so desperately needed. Danny reached for his phone and began scrolling through photos he had taken during happier times. Among them, he stumbled upon a picture of a serene beach up north, with the sun setting over the horizon. That was it. The inspiration he needed.

With newfound determination, Danny set his plan in motion. He returned to the table ready to have his lunch and even tell his dear friend his plan.

"My sweet boy, you were there a long time. No issues?" a smart-arse Albert insinuated.

"No Albert, rather inspiration. I will share after our meal where my mind went to, and here comes Marie with our garlic bread and salad. Let's dig in."

The avocado salad was a simple plate of sliced avocados, a smattering of finely cut onions and small cherry tomatoes sprinkled with a few flecks of parmesan cheese. Strange, but Danny knew that the *'White Sheep'* pub chef was not your ordinary pub cook. *"Just look at the menu selection,"* Danny thought. Who would think a pub would have pan-fried abalone with zucchini and garlic as a lunch special?

The fish arrived before they could finish the garlic bread and it looked just wonderful and the aroma was divine just in itself. Serve in a deep dish, the juices just surrounded the fish fillets, and the poor abalone was quickly devoured.

"Now that was an excellent choice if I do not say so myself, which I did," cracking one of his silly laughs, said Albert.

"Now what was this epiphany you arrived to in the toilet?"

"Let's order a sherry before I start, OK?"

"I never say no to alcohol darling, you know me," as Albert waves to Marie, who came over, took the order for two Harvey Bristol Cream drinks, which does not take her long to deliver.

After taking a sip, Danny starts.

"Albert, I need some time off. Away from *'Village Books & Stuff,'* not here for our new venture *'Locks & Loaded'* I need time to relax and see what I need to do to get over this failure with Alessia."

"I see," said Albert, gulping his sherry down, surprised at Danny's statement. "Where and for how long, my sweet boy, are you thinking of going?"

Danny takes out his phone and shows Albert his inspiration photo.

"Nice. So, you were there before?"

"Yes, a long time ago, before I purchase the bookshop. I am sure it has changed a bit, but I loved it and I'm sure I could rent a small place on the beach for a couple of months and just get my head on straight."

Albert does not say a word for what seems like an eternity, which was very unusual for him, but Danny waited patiently for his friend to think and respond.

"Danny, my darling, all I ever want for you is to be happy. I know you hired that young, delicious young Peter to help you run *Village Books & Stuff* and from our past conversations, he is doing a wonderful job. A little promotion from assistant manager to manager, a slight boost in his salary, and he will do an even more wonderful job for you while you are away. So that part of your business is covered. Our other business interests in *Ophelia's Pink Petals Flower Shop* and *Petite Maison* will continue going well when you are away, and I will, of course, keep you posted on how *'Locks & Loaded'* is going. I want you to be at the grand opening of *'Locks & Loaded.'* You will be there, right? You do not plan to leave before then?"

"Of course I will be there. I said I would be, and I always keep my word. I will leave afterwards."

You could see a sigh of relief from Albert. He knew that the grand opening was important for us both and we had decided on *'Locks & Loaded'* as the name for this joint venture one evening at *'Petite Maison'* where the wine flowed all night long and, well, we got loaded, and somehow that stuck in our mind and thus *'Locks & Loaded'* was born.

"Oh, look at the time. I must be going. I have some people to meet. See you soon and I will let you know about the mayor as soon as I hear," Albert gets up and places a quick peek on Danny's cheek and, as always, leaves him with the bill.

Needing more time to think, Danny gives Marie a quick gesture showing his sherry drink, and she quickly brought another one.

After the grand opening and after taking care of Peter's promotion to manager at *'Village Books & Stuff,'* he would pack a few bags, leave behind his comfort zone, and embark on a journey up north to that tranquil beach. There, he hoped to find himself, to reconnect with the person he used to be before life's challenges had weighed him down.

Danny picks a serviette and starts making a list of things to bring: a notebook to jot down his thoughts, a guitar to serenade the waves, and a few books that had long gathered dust on his bookshelf at home. With each item he added, he felt a sense of purpose returning to his life.

He was determined to shed the weight of his worries, learn from his mistakes, and, most importantly, rediscover the joy in the simple things that had once made him feel truly alive.

Marie comes back with the bill and a quick look at it made him smile.

"You are going to miss this, dear Albert. Who is going to pay for your meals when I am not here?" Danny smiled to himself, feeling no longer uncertain.

Chapter Two – Grand Opening

The day finally arrived for the grand opening of *Locks & Loaded* in the bustling heart of the CBD of Newport. Main Street exudes a posh and picturesque vibe in Northport with its fashionable boutiques and chic cafes, creating a sense of anticipation in the air. The city's fashion elite, celebrities and tastemakers had all gathered for the grand opening of *Locks & Loaded*, a name that will quickly become synonymous with glamour and luxury. The night was alive with whispers of excitement, and the venue itself was a testament to opulence.

Albert and Danny purchased a historic building, meticulously restored to its former grandeur. The facade was adorned with glistening gold accents, and an enchanting marquee spelled out the salon's name in elegant cursive. A crimson carpet stretched from the entrance to the street, providing a pathway for the city's elite to make their grand entrance.

As the evening sun dipped below the horizon, the first guests arrived, and they emerged from sleek black cars and walked the scarlet carpet with a grace that seemed inherent to their status. Paparazzi snapped photos of the glamorous arrivals, and they filled the air with the flash of cameras and the murmur of the crowd.

Inside, the salon was a vision of beauty. Albert had gone all out, and Danny did not mind.

Crystal chandeliers dangled from the ceiling, casting a soft, warm glow over the marble floors and plush velvet seating. Giant mirrors lined the walls, reflecting the intricate coiffures of the salon's stylists, who were artfully tending to their clients. The scent of exotic perfumes mingled with the subtle aroma of freshly brewed coffee, creating an intoxicating ambiance.

The highlight of the evening was, of course, Albert, who described himself as a visionary in the world of hairstyling. He is an icon of elegance himself, with his perfectly coiffed blond hair, his outlandish outfit, and his poise that commanded attention. Albert moved through the crowd, greeting the guests with charm and grace, his smile radiating the passion he has for his craft, and the six champagne drinks also smooth the way for him.

Throughout the night, there were live demonstrations by the salon's ten top stylists. They transformed their clients, each a blank canvas, into works of art. The stylists performed live demonstrations throughout the night, crafting elaborate updos, intricate braids and luscious curls with the precision of a maestro. This garnered gasps of admiration from the onlookers.

As the evening wore on, the energy of the grand opening continued to high crescendo. Guests mingled and chatted, sipping on champagne and sampling delectable canapés created by a renowned chef. Every moment he could, Albert would address the crowd, expressing his gratitude for their presence and his vision for *Locks & Loaded* as a sanctuary for beauty and style in the city.

The night culminated with a fashion show, where models strutted down a catwalk displaying innovative hairstyles, with each look a testament to the creativity and expertise of the salon's talented stylists.

As the last model took her bow and the applause filled the room, Albert stood at the end of the catwalk, a gleam of pride in his eyes. *Locks & Loaded* had officially opened its doors to the world, and it was clear that it would become a beacon of luxury, a place where beauty and glamour intersected. The grand opening was not just a celebration of a salon but a celebration of elegance and creativity, marking the beginning of a new era in the world of hairstyling.

Danny stood to the side, watching all of this, and with his drink in hand, he was actually enjoying himself, especially as he watched Albert take control of the crowd. He raised his glass of his favourite beer, Great Northern Super Crisp, to Albert and sees Albert's smile turned into a frown and Danny feels a tap on the shoulder and he turns and sees Detective Malcolm Cassell grinning at him.

"So much for a grand opening," Danny thinks to himself.

Chapter Three – Crystal Cove

Danny turns and finds Detective Malcolm Cassell wearing a smile that is a mix of amusement and confidence. "Well, Monk, you really know how to put on a show. Must have cost a bundle."

"You're not doing too bad yourself, Senior Detective Cassell," he replied, his voice a smooth purr. "I hear your promotion came through last month."

Cassell raised an eyebrow, intrigued by the audacity of the master thief. "Oh, really? And how did you hear about it?"

"From Chief Inspector Wendy Montague, we keep in touch, you know."

"I see, so you and the Chief Inspector are still a 'thing'?"

"No Cassell, we are not a 'thing.' We just ran into each other at a function a while back and you came up in the conversation. Not sure why, but you did. Still catching criminals?"

Cassell again smiled with those good teeth of his and takes a gulp of his champagne.

"Again, I must say you must have spent a bundle here. How much does this champagne go per bottle? $10, $20 dollars?"

"No, Senior Detective Cassell, this drop is a bit more expensive than what you mentioned. It is a Veuve Clicquot Cave Privée Brut 1980 with a wonderful palate that is steely and youthful, with tight minerality and hints of smokiness and flint. It has a blend of 53% Pinot noir, 37% Chardonnay and 10% Pinot Meunier."

Cassell places his glass on a table and grumbles something that sounded like: "Give me a VB any time."

world, and it was clear that it would become a beacon of luxury, a place where beauty and glamour intersected. The grand opening was not just a celebration of a salon but a celebration of elegance and creativity, marking the beginning of a new era in the world of hairstyling.

Danny stood to the side, watching all of this, and with his drink in hand, he was actually enjoying himself, especially as he watched Albert take control of the crowd. He raised his glass of his favourite beer, Great Northern Super Crisp, to Albert and sees Albert's smile turned into a frown and Danny feels a tap on the shoulder and he turns and sees Detective Malcolm Cassell grinning at him.

"So much for a grand opening," Danny thinks to himself.

Chapter Three – Crystal Cove

Danny turns and finds Detective Malcolm Cassell wearing a smile that is a mix of amusement and confidence. "Well, Monk, you really know how to put on a show. Must have cost a bundle."

"You're not doing too bad yourself, Senior Detective Cassell," he replied, his voice a smooth purr. "I hear your promotion came through last month."

Cassell raised an eyebrow, intrigued by the audacity of the master thief. "Oh, really? And how did you hear about it?"

"From Chief Inspector Wendy Montague, we keep in touch, you know."

"I see, so you and the Chief Inspector are still a 'thing'?"

"No Cassell, we are not a 'thing.' We just ran into each other at a function a while back and you came up in the conversation. Not sure why, but you did. Still catching criminals?"

Cassell again smiled with those good teeth of his and takes a gulp of his champagne.

"Again, I must say you must have spent a bundle here. How much does this champagne go per bottle? $10, $20 dollars?"

"No, Senior Detective Cassell, this drop is a bit more expensive than what you mentioned. It is a Veuve Clicquot Cave Privée Brut 1980 with a wonderful palate that is steely and youthful, with tight minerality and hints of smokiness and flint. It has a blend of 53% Pinot noir, 37% Chardonnay and 10% Pinot Meunier."

Cassell places his glass on a table and grumbles something that sounded like: "Give me a VB any time."

Danny takes a closer look at Senior Detective Cassell. Instead of his usual medium charcoal hue suit that looks so-so good with a rumpled white dress shirt and a slim dark tie, Cassell was wearing a pretty spiff three-piece suit, making Cassell exude a sense of timeless elegance and sophistication. *"Quite a change,"* thought Danny. *"Maybe he hit the lotto?"*

"You look spiffy tonight, Cassell. On a date?"

His teeth again shine through and Cassell gives Danny a look that reminded Danny that he should always tread carefully with Cassell, even though he and Albert are no longer in the 'acquisition business.'

"Just making sure you and Guzman are staying out of trouble. Things have been quite slow in the larceny department these past seven to ten months. I guess some folks just got bored and decided that cutting hair is more exciting. Right, Monk?"

"There you have it. After us for our past acquisitions. The man is like a dog with a bone," was all Danny could think.

"You still have Mr Guzman and me confused with someone else. We are law-abiding citizens and entrepreneurs. Even Chief Inspector Wendy Montague has so stated this to you frequently in the past and yet you cannot drop this notion. Why is that Cassell?"

"Because Monk, you, and that partner of yours Guzman, have fleeced so many with your activities and are living the good life of splendour and glamour. I will prove you two are crooks."

"Senior Detective Cassell, my, oh my, you look so nice," a soft female voice utters.

Both Danny and Cassell turn and there, wearing a breathtaking strapless evening gown, a masterpiece of sartorial artistry, is Chief Inspector Wendy Montague. Her gown was a deep midnight blue, its luxurious fabric cascading gracefully from her shoulders to the floor. It hugged her hourglass figure in all the right places, accentuating her natural beauty.

The neckline of the gown was tastefully adorned with intricate beading, adding a touch of opulence to the otherwise sleek and understated design. The strapless bodice, which was expertly crafted for a perfect fit, beautifully accentuated her collarbones and shoulders. With its flared A-line silhouette, the gown embodied a hint of classic Hollywood glamour.

Her fine hairdo was a testament to her diligence. Someone had artfully styled her dark tresses into a timeless chignon, with tendrils of hair gently framing her face. The updo was flawlessly executed, not a single strand out of place, and it added an air of regal elegance to her overall look. A single sparkling hairpin, adorned with a precious gemstone, held the chignon in place, catching the light and creating a subtle, dazzling focal point.

Completing her ensemble, she wore delicate diamond earrings that glinted with every move, and a pair of elegant stiletto heels that elongated her legs and added a touch of allure to her stride. Her makeup was impeccable, with soft, smoky eyes and a classic red lips that enhanced her natural beauty without overpowering it.

"Chief Inspector Wendy Montague, so nice to see you. So glad you accepted the invitation. The senior detective and I were just speaking about you," said Danny with a big smile on his face, looking straight at Cassell.

"Were you now? Nothing but good things, I supposed. You boys are behaving? This is not the time nor place for past animosities between you both. Besides, those days are behind you both. Correct?"

"They are in my book Chief Inspector Wendy Montague," answers Danny, with Cassell not answered one way or another.

Grabbing Danny's arms, Chief Inspector Wendy Montague moves him away from Cassell. "Come, Mr Monk, let's mingle a bit," and she leaves Cassell standing there.

"Well, Chief Inspector Wendy Montague, I am sure you pissed off Senior Detective Cassell just now."

With a smile on her face, the answer surprised Danny.

"Tough shit. He is a big boy and should know when to stop chasing wild allegations. Now, let's get me a drink and tell me what you have been up to since the last time we spent time together."

"I am surprised Laura Barton did not come with you, Wendy."

"She is with her father, working in New York on a new project. She sends you her best, as always," with a slight wink.

"I am sure she does," was the only thing Danny could respond with.

With the Chief in his arms, Danny felt that the evening would go on as well as possible with Cassell kept at bay. At least for the time being.

"Oh darling. What a beautiful frock. Where did you find such a divine gown?"

That comment came from Albert, who, after seeing Cassell tap Danny on the shoulder, had been socialising with his guests until now.

"This little thing? I got it at Versace in the city. Saw it and had to have it and then what better place to show it off than at your grand opening? Do you agree?" as Wendy does a twirl for both Danny and Albert to enjoy her dress and Danny her figure, mostly.

"Oh, look, there is the Lord Mayor of Northport. Let me call in on her. See you boys."

As Wendy trails off to meet the lord mayor Albert cannot help but remark: "Well, she seems in a great mood. She still has a thing for you, right, Danny?"

"No sure Albert. Remember, she and Laura were, how shall I say it, adventurous. Much more adventurous than me."

"Aha," is all Albert said and then he asked: "What was that awful man Cassell up to? Can he not leave us alone? We are no longer in the business of acquisitions."

"I know Albert, but remember, the police solved none of those crimes. The cases are still opened, so he is looking for another feather in his cap."

"After all we did for him, helping him solve the murder of the Randolph's cleaner. How ungrateful of him."

"Well, he got a promotion out of it, so he is happy, I guess," Danny said.

"Ungrateful ocker, which is what he is. Let's forget about him. The night has been a success, Danny. Thanks for letting me go just wild. I am so happy. You are a darling," and smacks a quick peck on Danny's cheek.

Danny was happy as well.

He loved that he was able to make this evening a grand evening for him. He deserved it. Albert has been there for Danny. Through the challenging times when he almost lost village Books & Stuff to the misadventures they endured together in the acquisition business, as Albert called it.

Danny was static that the evening has been a success.

Now came the hard part. When to tell Albert he would leave for Crystal Cove in a month.

Chapter Four – The Best

Tuesday morning, Danny opened *Village Books & Stuff* right on time. The soft chime of the doorbell always signals the start of another day in the cosy bookstore. He quickly busied himself with the tasks at hand, straightening shelves and checking inventory, all the while glancing at his watch. Time was ticking, and he needed to hurry.

At 10 AM, Peter, his newly appointed store manager, was supposed to come in to take over the daily operations while he was away. Danny was confident in Peter's abilities, but he couldn't help feeling a pang of nostalgia as he realised this was the last morning he would run the shop. Well, at least for a while. He had to hit the road to Crystal Cove by 2 PM, with a quick stopover night at Taree, but there was one important thing he needed to do before that.

Danny planned to have a farewell lunch with Albert and give him the news of his departure. Feeling guilty about giving Albert the notice at the last minute, Danny thought it was the best way to avoid Albert going on and on about being left behind. Albert would describe it as *"leaving me behind like a dog."*

No matter the preparation, Albert would never fathom the possibility that his friend would leave his side.

As the morning flew by, Danny was antsy with anticipation. The clock finally struck 10 AM, and Peter walked through the door with a warm smile. "You can count on me, Danny," Peter assured him. "I've got everything under control here."

Now came the hard part. When to tell Albert he would leave for Crystal Cove in a month.

Chapter Four – The Best

Tuesday morning, Danny opened *Village Books & Stuff* right on time. The soft chime of the doorbell always signals the start of another day in the cosy bookstore. He quickly busied himself with the tasks at hand, straightening shelves and checking inventory, all the while glancing at his watch. Time was ticking, and he needed to hurry.

At 10 AM, Peter, his newly appointed store manager, was supposed to come in to take over the daily operations while he was away. Danny was confident in Peter's abilities, but he couldn't help feeling a pang of nostalgia as he realised this was the last morning he would run the shop. Well, at least for a while. He had to hit the road to Crystal Cove by 2 PM, with a quick stopover night at Taree, but there was one important thing he needed to do before that.

Danny planned to have a farewell lunch with Albert and give him the news of his departure. Feeling guilty about giving Albert the notice at the last minute, Danny thought it was the best way to avoid Albert going on and on about being left behind. Albert would describe it as *"leaving me behind like a dog."*

No matter the preparation, Albert would never fathom the possibility that his friend would leave his side.

As the morning flew by, Danny was antsy with anticipation. The clock finally struck 10 AM, and Peter walked through the door with a warm smile. "You can count on me, Danny," Peter assured him. "I've got everything under control here."

Relieved and grateful for Peter's support, Danny started going over all the last details about the store.

Peter just smiles. As assistant manager, Peter has watched the store for many months now and knew the routine by heart. He also knew that leaving your baby in the care of a babysitter is hard, or so said Peter's mother to him many a time.

Looking at his watch, Danny realised he had to go, and grabbed his coat and shook Peter's hands and stepped out the front door and took one last look at his store. Danny almost wanted to wave goodbye to the familiar sights of the bookstore. With a hint of sadness, he made his way to the *White Sheep*, where he and Albert had shared countless meals and memories.

As he entered the pub, he spotted Albert sitting at their usual corner table, engrossed in his mobile phone. Danny approached him with a smile and sat down. "Hey, Albert," he said with a hint of excitement in his voice.

Albert looks up, puts down his mobile, and gives Danny a big smile. "Danny, darling, I'm starving. Why are you so late?"

A quick glance at his watch and he sees the time is 12: OO PM, right on time. *"Albert is always such a prima donna,"* Danny thought, smiled to himself.

Danny leaned in closer, his voice low. "I have a little secret to share with you, my friend."

"Oh goody, gossip. I love it. Tell me all sweetness," was Albert's response.

Albert's eyes widened as Danny reveals his plans to head to Crystal Cove by the afternoon. The news leaves Albert both surprised, sad, and touched. He knew how much this journey was needed by Danny and how much it meant to him, and while he did not want Danny to leave, he couldn't help but smile.

"You naughty boy, keeping this from me!" Albert chuckled. "I'm going to miss you, my sugariness, but I understand. It is like Crystal Cove has been calling your name. Am I right?"

"It has Albert. I need this break. All is set with the store, with Peter handling it all for me while I am away. You OK with *Locks & Loaded*?"

"Of course, darling. When is Albert not able to handle the work?"

"Do you actually work, Albert? I thought you supervised the staff," Danny interjected with a big grin.

"Silly boy, silly boy. Supervising is work, fun work, for sure. Someone has to manage, and that is Moi! Now what's for lunch?" handing Danny the menu.

As always, the *White Sheep* daily specials look more like a 5-star restaurant than pub food. This time Albert speaks first and suggests that they go for the slow-roasted lamb with skordalia with a creamy sauce made from garlic and potatoes.

"Albert, your suggestion is too filling and heavy of a meal for me. You go ahead, I will stick with just a plain Caesar salad with grilled chicken and some garlic bread. That should suffice for me and not put me to sleep on the road."

Albert nods and call over Marie who quickly takes the order, a bottle of MÉRITE's 2016 Q Merlot which will highlight the attributes of this wine intense fruit flavours, bright natural acidity, and fine tannins which will go simply fine with the lamb and the salad.

The conversations continued before, during, and after they received and finished the meal, and Danny waved to Maire to come over.

"Marie, I will have a double espresso," and looked at Albert to see if he wanted one.

"No, darling, you go right ahead with the coffee. I will have one of those after a meal sherry drink you like so much."

Maire looks at Danny and said: "Does he mean the Harvey Bristol Cream?"

Smiling, Danny nods.

"OK, a double espresso and one sherry coming right up."

"It's time Albert. I got to get going. It is past 2 PM and I want to reach Taree early to rest, have an early meal, a good restful sleep before heading to Crystal Cove."

"Did you make bookings at both places or are you just driving and seeing what happens?"

"No, I made booking at both places. A simple single room in Taree, but I booked a large B & B room at the Poplar Inn in Crystal Cove. It looked superb. Secluded, but close to the beach. I might do some swimming, fishing and do some boat chartering. Plenty to keep me busy and besides, I am bringing a couple of books to read."

"Of course, you are bringing books. You own a bookstore. Anything of interest I might look into?"

"You Albert. You read? I never seen you pick up a book before."

"I could start now that I will be all alone, like a dog left behind, now that you are leaving."

"Well, if you decide to read something, there is this local author J. F. Nodar who has two novels out which are quite interesting."

Albert looks at Danny with an inquisitive look: "Well...."

"Well, what Albert?"

"What are the titles of these novels? You do not expect me to do research, do you?"

"One of the novels has the title *Books, Pens & Larceny* and the other one, his new science fiction goes with the title *The Universe Between Us.*"

"Oh, my, they sound serious."

Danny looks at Albert as if to say the title does not make the books serious, but he goes ahead with another suggestion.

"Albert, the author has five anthology books out with funny short stories and poetry. His latest is *Stories to Share with My Partner – Book 5,* which is the one you should start with."

"Easy reading? You know I cannot delve into heavy stuff, darling."

"Yes, Albert. Light reading."

"In that case, I will drop by *Village Books & Stuff* and pick up a copy of all of them. You better be right, sweetie, or I will return them to the store."

"You know you cannot do that," Danny said, laughed a bit.

"I know, but I am trying to be assertive now that I will be left behind like a dog."

"*Oh, yes,*" Danny thought, "*a world class exaggeration prima donna.*"

"Danny, when are you coming back, sweetie?"

Danny busted laughed.

"I have not left yet, settled in Crystal Cove, got my head straighten out and you ask me when I am returning. You are something else, Albert."

Marie arrived with the espresso and sherry and places them in front of Danny and Albert.

As Danny sirs his coffee, Albert gulps his drink down.

Albert responds to Danny, continuing the conversation, with: "Yes, I am dear, and you know it. How about another drink before you leave?" and Albert waves his hand, showing two fingers at Marie, who understands the signal and nods back to Albert.

"Now listen, you can drink all you want, but I'm driving almost five hours to Taree and stopping for the day and then heading off in the morning. No more alcohol for me."

Danny gets up from his chair and walks around and gives Albert a quick peck on his forehead and walks out of the *White Sheep*.

Marie comes to the table with two drinks and Albert just points to his placemat and places both drinks down.

It hits Albert.

"Danny has left, and the sweet thing has saddled me with the cheque," he thinks to himself. *"Well, after all, Danny learned from the best,"* as Albert savours his drink and tackles his mobile phone once again.

Chapter Five - Barby

Embarking on a journey that Danny hopes will settle all his uncertainty once and for all and go ahead with his life he looks at his apartment for the last time, turns on his security alarm and walks down to his new sporty red metallic BMW 840i convertible. Danny thought he was crazy in purchasing a car. He rarely went anywhere and when he did he either drive his old car or Uber it, but with money in the bank from his share of the acquisition profits, he figured he could spoil himself with a new car, an expensive car, at that. Danny was taking enough clothes to fit in two medium size suitcases and the boot had plenty of room for them. He also put a small cooler in the back with some ice and water bottles in case he got thirsty and just needed a quick pit stop. Before taking off, he admires his purchase. *"Now let's see how you do on the open road for the $230,000 I spent on you,"* Danny thought as he sat in it, turned on the ignition, and got ready to leave.

From Northport to Crystal Cove, Danny knew he was going to experience one of the most iconic of Australia's drives that will leave him, once again, enchanted with its picturesque beauty. Danny was ready to be captivated by the friendly little beach towns, ancient rainforests, and the most incredible coastline along the way.

As Danny leaves the charming and luscious rural atmosphere of Northport, the serene beauty of the Australian landscape immediately envelops him. Following the winding roads, any tourist would find themselves on the doorstep of one of the country's most incredible road trips.

Going north on, the M1 quickly realises he is already at Gosford and looks at his speedometer. *"No, I am going to the speed limit. I have not been speeding,"* he thinks to himself and smiled

Albert responds to Danny, continuing the conversation, with: "Yes, I am dear, and you know it. How about another drink before you leave?" and Albert waves his hand, showing two fingers at Marie, who understands the signal and nods back to Albert.

"Now listen, you can drink all you want, but I'm driving almost five hours to Taree and stopping for the day and then heading off in the morning. No more alcohol for me."

Danny gets up from his chair and walks around and gives Albert a quick peck on his forehead and walks out of the *White Sheep*.

Marie comes to the table with two drinks and Albert just points to his placemat and places both drinks down.

It hits Albert.

"Danny has left, and the sweet thing has saddled me with the cheque," he thinks to himself. *"Well, after all, Danny learned from the best,"* as Albert savours his drink and tackles his mobile phone once again.

Chapter Five - Barby

Embarking on a journey that Danny hopes will settle all his uncertainty once and for all and go ahead with his life he looks at his apartment for the last time, turns on his security alarm and walks down to his new sporty red metallic BMW 840i convertible. Danny thought he was crazy in purchasing a car. He rarely went anywhere and when he did he either drive his old car or Uber it, but with money in the bank from his share of the acquisition profits, he figured he could spoil himself with a new car, an expensive car, at that. Danny was taking enough clothes to fit in two medium size suitcases and the boot had plenty of room for them. He also put a small cooler in the back with some ice and water bottles in case he got thirsty and just needed a quick pit stop. Before taking off, he admires his purchase. *"Now let's see how you do on the open road for the $230,000 I spent on you,"* Danny thought as he sat in it, turned on the ignition, and got ready to leave.

From Northport to Crystal Cove, Danny knew he was going to experience one of the most iconic of Australia's drives that will leave him, once again, enchanted with its picturesque beauty. Danny was ready to be captivated by the friendly little beach towns, ancient rainforests, and the most incredible coastline along the way.

As Danny leaves the charming and luscious rural atmosphere of Northport, the serene beauty of the Australian landscape immediately envelops him. Following the winding roads, any tourist would find themselves on the doorstep of one of the country's most incredible road trips.

Going north on, the M1 quickly realises he is already at Gosford and looks at his speedometer. *"No, I am going to the speed limit. I have not been speeding,"* he thinks to himself and smiled because he seems to float in his new car. He has his Bowers & Wilkins Diamond surround sound system blasting away and yet it is not blaring even with the top down. *"Yes, you did good, Danny boy. Excellent choice,"* he said aloud.

Soon after Gosford, Danny sees the exit sign for the friendly little beach towns, each with its own unique character, like the laid-back vibe of Bonnells Bay and Pearl Beach in Wangi Wangi. *"No time to stop if I want to make it to Taree for the night,"* again he thinks to himself.

A bit of a traffic delay as he reached Newcastle since it is now close to rush hour and Danny slowed down to the traffic pattern and every so often got a smile and a thumbs up for a fellow driver as they appreciate it, or is it envy, of his new car.

Nature calls and Danny decides that the next little village he sees will be an ideal spot for a quick stop. Looking at his fuel gauge, he is Ok but decides that is always best to be safe so he will look for a petrol station, fill up and use the facilities as well. He sees the exit for Coolongolook and gets off the M1.

Driving through the small village, Danny spots the local Ampol petrol station, fills up and uses the facilities. As he goes to drive off, he notices a small café with the name The Salty Fish Shop and he drove into it with the thought of getting himself a coffee.

Danny went to the counter, ordered a double espresso and a glass of water from the older lady behind the counter and sat at a nearby table, picking up the menu to pass the time. A few minutes later, an elderly man arrived with both the water and the coffee for Danny and asks him about his destination.

"I am going to Crystal Cove for a few weeks, maybe months, just some me time."

"Never been but heard it's lovely there. Got yourself a place, or are you just renting?"

"Just renting. Hoping to relax a bit."

"I see," the elderly gentleman said as he turns, looks at the expensive car, and turns to Danny with a smile.

"Dropped a few on that one. Must be a single man."

Danny laughed and just nodded in the affirmative.

"Harold, are you bothering the gentleman? Let him be and have his coffee."

"Betty, I am not bothering him," he said, looking at Danny for support, which Danny then spoke up on and went to his defence really quick.

"No. he is no bother."

With a smile Harold mouths a 'thank you' and leaves.

"Harold, wait a second. I got a quick question."

"Sure, shoot."

"Why The Salty Fish Shop name for the store? I am simply curious. I glanced at the menu while waiting for the coffee and saw no fish at all on it."

"Well, we started out as a seafood café, but it turned out," and he leaned closer to Danny, "Betty was an awful cook when it came to fish, so we changed the menu to cakes, coffee and a few sandwiches. She is happy and so are the customers now," Harold stated with a big smile.

With a big smile of his own, Danny thanked both Harold and Betty and drove off, knowing that in every little corner of the world, there was always a story to be enjoyed.

Forty minutes later, Danny pulled off the road into Taree and quickly found his motel, checked in, got settled into his room and went to KFC across the street and got himself a bucket of fried chicken and a soft drink.

Getting comfortable, Danny turned on the TV, placed the chicken bucket on his lap and began to eat, and his mind reflected on the day and the drive.

The day had been long, but with pleasant experiences. First, he turns the store over to Peter. Then lunch with Albert went well and then the drive had no incidents. Danny thought of the sights, and people he met, and the memories of friendly towns, ancient rainforests, and the stunning Australian coastline. The drive is a testament to the natural beauty and diverse experiences that make Australia a paradise. He was reminded of the 1984 commercial pitched to the Americas by

Paul Hogan to come to the Land Down Under. *"Yes, I might just do like Paul Hogan said in the commercial and put another shrimp on the barby for any visitor from anywhere in the world!"*

Chapter Six – The Poplar Inn

Morning arrived and Danny had a quick shower and grabbed a coffee and a scone and was out the door by 9 AM. He had only five more hours until reaching Crystal Cove, and he wanted to arrive as soon as possible. He had requested an early check in and had received a promise that a room of his choice would be available upon his arrival. The drive went extremely well, with only one stop to rest at Maclean's *Coffeemania Café* for a quick espresso, a bathroom break and a twenty-minute walk around the area to stretch his legs.

After the break, it was only a short one hour and thirty minutes run and Danny arrived at Crystal Cove and quickly, thanks to his GPS, finds the Poplar Inn.

It is spectacular to say the least for the website photos gave it no justice.

The inn stood nestled on the outskirts of Crystal Cove, and its exterior had a charming blend of rustic and welcoming features. A well-worn cobblestone path leads guests to the front entrance, with a small wrought-iron lantern casting a warm, inviting glow in the early evening. The inn's façade is a combination of aged timber beams and whitewashed plaster, exuding a timeless, cosy feel. A large wooden sign with intricate, hand-painted lettering proudly displayed the inn's name, "The Poplar Inn," swinging gently in the breeze.

The owners must love flowers for flower boxes brimming with vibrant, seasonal blooms hang beneath the inn's windows, adding splashes of colour to the scene. The corrugated iron roof, though weathered, remains sturdy and gives the inn a classic countryside charm. Two wooden benches to sit on either side of the entrance, offering a place for weary travellers to rest and take in the serene surroundings, and Danny can hear the ocean's waves nearby.

Danny carried his suitcase in with him and just marvels at the interior. Again, photos sometimes do no justice to a place.

Inside, the space is a cosy haven adorned with exposed wooden beams on the ceiling. Oil paintings of beach landscapes and antique brass sconces adorn the walls, casting a soft, golden light. The scent of freshly polished wood mingled with the aroma of hearty, home-cooked meals. A large stone hearth dominates one wall, a roaring fire within casting flickering shadows that dance across the room. "It is spring and yet the fireplace just seems right," thought Danny as he continued looking around. The fireplace dominated one wall, casting flickering shadows that dance across the room. The arrangement of comfortable, well-worn leather armchairs and plush sofas around it invites guests to relax and unwind. A hand-knotted Persian rug covered the wide plank wooden floor, adding an element of luxury. *"Oh, I think I am already feeling just perfect here,"* again Danny thought.

Looking to his left, Danny saw the bar and dining area. The bar, made of rich mahogany, occupies a corner of the room. Bottles of aged spirits lined the shelves, and a wall of polished glass reflected the warm ambiance, making the space feel even more inviting. Taking a quick look into the dining area, Danny marvelled at the heavy oak tables and upholstered chairs. He observed each table was adorned with fresh flowers in vases and featured linen tablecloths and antique silverware. Soft, ambient music played in the background, creating a soothing atmosphere for a leisurely meal. *"I probably missed lunch, but dinner should be just great here,"* again was Danny's thought.

As Danny explored further, he discovered a nook with shelves stacked high with well-loved books and board games, providing guests with a quiet retreat for reading or friendly competition. Up a wooden staircase should be the rooms. Overall, the Poplar Inn offered a timeless blend of rustic charm and comfort that made Danny feel he had chosen well.

"Good afternoon. You must be Mr Monk," came a voice from behind Danny.

"My name is Gertie, co-owner of the Poplar Inn."

Danny turned and saw Gertie. She looked middle-aged but exuded a timeless elegance and hospitality that goes with the charming establishment. With chestnut hair cascading down to her shoulders and a face that carries a few well-earned laugh lines, Gertie possessed a radiant and welcoming beauty. Her eyes struck a shade of green, and they sparkled with genuine interest in her guests, and her smile was a beacon of warmth.

"Yes, I am Danny Monk. Pleasure to be here, Gertie."

"Who are you speaking with?" came a voice from behind the dining room said a man came toward them. The man, who had neatly combed greying hair, a salt and pepper beard, and a few distinguished lines etched onto his face, was standing there. He stood at an average height with a sturdy build that suggested years of arduous work. His warm, hazel eyes twinkle with a welcoming sincerity, and his smile matched the welcoming attitude of Gertie.

"Mr Monk, this is my husband, Samuel Bailey. We run the Poplar Inn along with our staff."

"A pleasure to meet you, Mr Monk," Samuel said, shaking Danny's hand.

"Likewise, sir."

"Oh, please, we are just Gertie and Samuel."

"OK, a pleasure to meet the both of you, Gertie, and Samuel. Call me Danny then."

"Well, Danny, come over to the reception counter and let me check you in and, like I said to you on the phone, I will let you have your choice of rooms to pick from," Gertie said.

"I'm going back to the kitchen, Gertie. Do you need help with your luggage, Danny?"

"No, I am OK, thanks Samuel."

Danny heads over the counter and Gertie gives him his options.

"Your first option is the Sea Breeze Suite. This suite has a spacious, open-concept room with a living area and a kitchenette. It boasts a large window that provides breathtaking panoramic views of the ocean. Guests can enjoy gentle sea breezes on the attached private deck. Your second choice is the Captain's Quarters is the most luxurious room in the inn, featuring a four-poster king-sized bed, a spacious sitting area, and a private fireplace. The room exudes a sense of maritime elegance, and it offers an unobstructed view of the ocean from a private balcony from which you can enjoy any of your room service meals. Do you have a preference?"

"What is the cost for the four weeks and remember, I might stay another month or two more?"

Gertie took out a sheet from a file and shows it to Danny.

"Danny, I remember our phone conversation, so I worked out a price for either room that you can see is based on the length of stay. For the four weeks, the Sea Breeze runs to $6,750 which includes breakfast in our dining room everyday while the Captains quarters runs for the same four weeks $8,250 including breakfast everyday plus you get one full breakfast delivered to your room once a week, as long as you let us know by noon the day before. Which do you prefer?"

Money was not an issue, so without hesitation, Danny chooses the Captain's Quarters and gave her his AMEX Platinum Metal card.

Danny thought he saw Gertie blink twice at the sight of the card, but she took it, ran it through and in seconds, the approval came through.

"Do you mind if I also take a card imprint for any future purchases at the bar and evening dinner?"

"No, please go ahead. I am sure I will use the facilities once or twice while I am here. While we are discussing food, is the restaurant open for lunch?"

"Sorry Danny, the restaurant opens for breakfast from 7 AM to 9:30 AM and then lunch from 11:30 AM until 2 PM. You just missed it; however, I can recommend a lovely café in Crystal Cove if you do not mind a ten-minute drive. It is right by the ocean with a lovely view, and they stay open till 6 PM serving food."

"That sounds great. What is the name and address?"

"The name is the Seashell Café and is on Shore Drive. You cannot miss it. If you have a GPS, just put in the street name and you will see it and tell Toni that we recommended the place."

"Excellent," as Danny grabbed his keys, and Gertie said to him.

"Danny, leave the luggage and get some food for yourself. I will get Robert to take them to your room. Go enjoy lunch, a drink and the beautiful ocean view of Crystal Cove."

"You convinced me, Gertie. Thanks, I will do exactly that," he said, dropping his bags next to the counter.

As Danny steps outside, the afternoon sun is still high in the sky, but Danny felt the ocean breezes and, with a big smile, he gets into his car and sets the GPS to Shore Drive.

Chapter Seven – The Seashell Café

Getting to the main part of Crystal Cove was easy, and Danny found the Seashell Café just as easy. Parking the car, he stepped out and looked at Crystal Cove main street. It has changed a lot since his last visit many years ago. There are a few more stores on the street and they are glittery and posher. *"I'll have a walk around town after lunch and scope it out,"* Danny thinks, and he hears the ocean waves caressing the shoreline behind the café. The smell of the ocean is just wonderful. *"Just what I need,"* thought Danny as he turns to look at the Seashell Café.

The Seashell Café exudes a welcoming charm.

Weathered cedar shingles adorn the exterior, painted in muted pastel hues of sea foam green and soft coral, giving it a rustic yet inviting appearance. A wrought-iron sign bearing the cafe's name announces its presence to any passersby.

Danny saw he could access the front entrance via a cobblestone path that wounded through a small garden adorned with colourful hydrangeas, beach daisies and aromatic herb pots. The owners placed a wooden fence at the entrance of the café, and they covered it with climbing roses. Acting like a shield against the coastal winds while giving the café a secluded atmosphere. Weathered driftwood benches and vintage lanterns line the path, inviting guests to linger and savour the tranquil seaside ambiance.

Danny waltzed in nonchalantly inside and found a cosy interior bathed in the warm glow of soft, amber-hued pendant lights that cast a comforting radiance throughout the space. They adorned the walls with reclaimed wood panelling, adorned with a smattering of nautical artefacts, such as ship wheels and vintage maritime maps. An old brass ship's bell, polished to a shine, hung near the entrance, a reminder of the cafe's seaside location.

The heart of the café features a handcrafted wooden bar with a worn, weathered finish, where patrons can sit on plush, leather barstools. Behind the bar, a collection of colourful glass bottles held an array of artisanal spirits and infusions. A Gaggia Americano 1957 vintage espresso machine hissed and steamed, filling the air with the rich scent of freshly brewed coffee.

Intimate wooden tables for two are scattered throughout the space, each adorned with flickering candles in hurricane lanterns and draped with chequered tablecloths. Soft jazz music filled the air, setting a soothing backdrop for conversations and contemplation. An open fireplace, built from local stone, crackles warmly during the cooler seaside evenings.

Looking at the rear of the café, large windows provide unobstructed views of Crystal Cove and the gently rolling waves. White lace curtains, gently swaying in the breeze, frame these picturesque views, adding to the cafe's intimate and inviting atmosphere. The sound of seagulls and the salty sea breeze waft in, creating a sensory connection to the seaside setting.

This intimate, cosy seaside cafe is a tranquil oasis where locals and tourists can savour a cup of coffee, enjoy a freshly baked pastry, and lose themselves in the soothing ambiance of the sea. Danny felt he struck gold with Crystal Cove, the Poplar Inn and now the Seashell Café.

"Take any table luv, I'll be with you shortly," said a woman in her sixties, exuding a warm and welcoming aura as she stood behind the counter of the cosy cafe. Her salt and pepper hair framed her face, adding a touch of sophistication to her appearance. Her expressive brown eyes sparkled with a hint of wisdom, and her smile was as inviting as the aroma of freshly brewed coffee that enveloped the cafe.

Danny could see she wore a floral-printed apron that tied snugly around her waist, adding a cheerful and rustic charm to her attire. The apron bore the marks of her culinary adventures, hinting at the countless cups of coffee and delicious pastries she had served over the years. A subtle smudge of cocoa and a sprinkle of flour adorned the apron.

Coming over, she hands Danny the menu.

"Anything in particular you are hungry for, luv?"

"Not really," answers Danny with a smile on his face. "You have any recommendations?"

"You hungry or just want a nibble?"

"Good question," thought Danny. "I'm peckish, so something light."

"The chef has a wonderful variation of a Cuban Medianoche sandwich," pointing to the menu, "which she calls Mediodia, and is quite similar to the Medianoche sandwich but she adds her own blend of garlic aioli which gives it quite a slight variation. It has roast pork, bread, and butter pickles, Swiss cheese delivered to you in a challah roll. Quite delicious. It is my favourite."

"OK, that sounds OK. Let's go with that. And how about a lemon, lime and bitters to go with it?"

"I will bring them both right up," as she takes the menu and goes to place the order.

Danny glanced around the café and saw the place was still pretty busy. Almost all the tables are occupied, and the customers are mostly enjoying drinks and coffee. Occasionally, someone places a slice of cake on a fork, bringing a smile to their face.

The Seashell Café seems to be operated with a relatively small staff for, besides the woman who took his order, Danny sees two other ladies working the table and one barista. Looking to see if he can see into the kitchen, he saw movement but cannot determine how many more staff were in the kitchen, but he would assume at least two to three.

The sandwich arrived promptly, and its presentation was quite interesting. On his plate there was a pressed and grilled sandwich with a crusty, golden-brown exterior. The inside featured layers of the roast pork, Swiss cheese, pickles and Danny can see the garlic aioli dripping on its side. The sandwich reveals the layers of ingredients as it arrives cut into halves.

As for the smell, this variation of a Cuban sandwich offered an enticing aroma of roasted pork, melted cheese, and the enticing combination of the garlic aioli. This variation of a Cuban sandwich presented an enticing aroma. The chef crisped the bread up in butter, giving it a golden look is a masterpiece to look at. It came with a small side of white rice and black beans with small cut white onions sprinkled on the beans.

"I added the rice and beans," said the lady. "Complements of the house. Enjoy."

"Why thank you. It looks wonderful."

Danny ate the sandwich and delighted in the flavour. The garlic aioli was flavourful but not overwhelmingly garlicky, enhancing the sweetness of the pork. The cheese, while melted, was not gooey and added a wonderful flavour to the sandwich. Danny found the complimentary rice and black beans to be an unexpected bonus that filled him up.

"Well, you devoured that. Must have been hungrier than you thought, eh?"

Danny smiled at the lady and gave her his response: "I have to admit, it completely surprised me at how tasteful the sandwich was, and the rice and beans just made for a perfect pairing. My complements to the chef."

"Oh, I'm not the chef. My name is Cecilia. I am her mother; Toni is the chef. We are co-owners of the café. She is helping me out because our normal cook called in sick but should be in tomorrow. Hold on. I will get her and let you pay your complements in person."

Danny drank the last of his lemon, lime, and bitters and waits for Cecilia to returned with the chef and when she does, Danny had to do a double take.

Toni walked toward Danny, and she was wearing her chef's outfit, and the woman resembled a young Gina Lollobrigida. In her chef's outfit, Toni possessed a classic and timeless beauty with well-defined features and a sense of elegance. Her dark hair, neatly tied up in a bun glimmering with the light. She had striking and expressive eyes, which Danny found beautifully alluring. Her sculpted cheekbones added to her overall elegance. Her lips were full, sensuous and had a sultry appeal. Even with the chef's outfit, Danny can see her curvaceous and hourglass-shaped figure, and yet she carried herself with grace, poise and sophistication.

What struck Danny the most is the radiant smile. Toni had a bright, engaging smile that just relaxes anyone I her presence.

"Hi, I'm Toni. I hear you like my sandwich. I am so glad."

Danny is almost speechless but quickly recovers and stands up and introduces himself.

"Yes I did. My name is Danny Monk and Gertie, from the Poplar Inn, told me the café had excellent food at this time of the day and she was correct. Not only it was excellent, but I would describe it more than excellent. Outstanding would be better."

"Well, I'm glad you enjoyed it, Mr Monk. I hope that will encourage you to come back and even do a review of our little café on Google."

"Yes, I am sure I will return, and you can count on that review, Miss...?

"Antonia Webster, but everyone in town calls me Toni."

"And all my friends call me Danny," extending his hand.

Toni takes it and shakes Danny's hand and there seems to be electricity in their touch.

After what seems like an eternity of embarrassment, they drop the handshake and Toni said: "Well, nice to meet you Danny. Got to get back to work. Will see you around Crystal Cove."

"Yes you will. I am staying for a while, just enjoying some time off."

With a big smile Toni turned and returned to the kitchen and Danny walked to the counter and handed Cecilia his AMEX card.

"She is one good sandwich maker," Danny said to Cecilia.

"You should come back if she has to cover again. Her fish recipes are to die for. She is one heck of a chef."

"I will, I am sure of it," and Danny turned and headed out of the café.

"What the hell just happen," he thought to himself.

This Toni just knocked him off his balance. Is he ready for anything now in the way of a new friendship?

Danny's eyes just look down the Shore Drive and wonders to himself what this stay at Crystal Cove might bring.

Chapter Eight – Shore Drive

Danny looked at his watch. 3:30 PM. As stores close early in Australia except for any late night trading days, he hoped they might still be open, so Danny started a leisurely stroll from the café towards the rest of the stores on Shore Drive and checked out the rest of Crystal Cove on foot.

Crystal Cove changed a lot since his last visit. From a sleepy little village, it now has turned itself into a charming and picturesque seaside village with a street that winds its way along the tranquil coastline. Offering a delightful shopping experience for its newly found affluent tourist and newer residents. This scenic thoroughfare exudes an aura of elegance and sophistication, perfectly in tune with the tastes of a new influx of well-heeled clientele.

Lined with cobblestone pavements and adorned with vintage streetlamps ready to light up the night sky when it arrived. The street offered a nostalgic, old-world charm. As the salty breeze wafted in from the nearby sea, the street was often filled with the melodic sounds of seagulls and the gentle lapping of waves, creating a soothing atmosphere.

The focal point of this street is the row of six posh retail stores, each one meticulously designed to cater to the discerning tastes of the town's affluent visitors. The storefronts were adorned with large glass windows, framed with ornate ironwork, and draped with billowing, elegant curtains. Plush awnings protect shoppers from the occasional seaside drizzle, adding a touch of opulence to the storefronts.

The first store Danny saw was a high-end fashion boutique, displaying the latest designer clothing and accessories. Its window displayed feature mannequins dressed in the most stylish ensembles, while management adorned the interior with crystal chandeliers and luxurious fitting rooms. It had a simple store name: *Donatella's Boutique*.

Next door, an exquisite jewellery store gleamed with sparkling gems and precious metals. In its windows Danny could see velvet-lined display cases highlighting stunning necklaces, rings and timepieces, and but no prices, a hint of the adage. *'If you have to ask, you cannot afford it.'* A quick look at the store name tells Danny you need money to come in: *Platinum Elegance Jewellers*.

Continuing down the street, a gourmet delicatessen offers a curated selection of rare and imported culinary delights. The store is a sensory feast, with the aroma of freshly baked bread, artisanal cheeses and fine wines wafting from within. It also came with quite a unique name for the store: *Gourmet Gastronomy*.

Next to the delicatessen was a boutique art gallery. Danny could see from the window works from local artists. The gallery's well-lit interiors and carefully arranged exhibits provided an ideal backdrop for art collectors to browse and purchase exceptional pieces. Again, Danny notice that the one seascape on its window had the artist's name but no price. Danny notices the store's name and wonders if all these store owners got together and picked their store names together, for this one went by: *The Whimsical Palette*.

Further down the row, a luxury home decor store beckoned with its array of elegant furnishings and decorative items. Exquisite, handcrafted furniture, fine China and opulent textiles adorn the showroom, and while the furniture store might seem a bit out of place, or so thought Danny, the items in the store would blend with any of the ocean view homes and Danny was sure that the Poplar Inn purchased some of their furniture here. It had a normal name: *Haverty's*.

Mixed into this potpourri of stores was a high-end spa and wellness centre. It was massive in floor space, and Danny was sure by the name it had to be one of the national chains: *Fitness Fusion Nation*.

The last store was the smallest, but Danny thought it was the best. Looking at his watch, Danny notices it is 4: 20 PM, and the store is now closed, but he knew he had to come back and look inside. The name was as simple as it was wonderful to roll off his tongue: *Crystal Cove Bookshop.*

As Danny stood at the edge of the road, he surveyed the traffic, waiting for a safe moment to cross. Finally, spotting a break in the traffic, Danny briskly crossed the road. *"Can you believe it? There is a small rush hour in Crystal Cove. Who would have thought,"* Danny thought.

As he made his way to the other side, he couldn't help but notice a stark contrast in the calibre of the retail stores. The shops here were noticeably less posh than the ones he had just left behind. The storefronts were simpler, with signs and advertisements that lacked the high-end aesthetic of the previous block.

Upon closer inspection, Danny counted six more stores on this side of the road. Among them was an IGA supermarket, a no-frills grocery store known for its affordability and practicality. Next to it stood a petrol station, offering the convenience of fuel and snacks to passing motorists.

The remaining stores were a mix of local businesses, offering services ranging from a small electronic store, a hardware store, a dry-cleaning store, and a burger takeaway shop. Danny couldn't help but appreciate the diversity of these businesses, each catering to a distinct set of needs and preferences. Continuing his stroll down this side of the road, he reflected on the striking differences between the two blocks.

As he reached the next street, Danny looked but saw that the residential area of Crystal Cove was just starting and kept walking to inspect the neighbourhood.

Danny strolled through the middle-class neighbourhood, walking down streets lined with trees, each house possessing its own charm and character. The neighbourhood exuded a sense of comfort and community, with well-kept lawns, friendly neighbours and a cosy ambiance. He first noticed a charming cottage with a white picket fence. It had a warm, pastel-coloured exterior and flower boxes beneath the windows gave it a welcoming and quaint appearance. The well-tended garden featured blooming roses, and a neatly trimmed hedge.

A few homes after that, he came upon a classic colonial-style home. It had a brick façade, a symmetrical design and a beautiful front porch with white columns. The manicured front yard displayed a flagpole with an Australian flag fluttering in the breeze.

Then three houses near to the colonial, he saw a single-storey contemporary ranch-style house. Its clean lines, large windows and a minimalist front yard offered a more modern aesthetic. The residents had a well-maintained vegetable garden along the side of the house, demonstrating a commitment to sustainable living.

Still fascinated at the variety of homes, he found a stunning Victorian era house struck him with intricate gingerbread trim, turrets, and ornate detailing. The owners painted the house in vibrant colours, with stained glass windows that caught the sunlight. It was a true architectural gem in the neighbourhood.

Danny looked at his watch: 6:00 PM, *"Just a few more,"* he thought to himself as he noticed a practical split-level home. Its design provided a sense of spaciousness with multiple levels and a well-kept lawn. The garage featured two cars, and the driveway had three artfully arranged children's bicycles, hinting at a family living inside.

The last home on the street really stood out because of an eclectic character. A craftsman-style home with a mix of architectural elements, it had a porch adorned with handmade wooden crafts. The yard was filled with a variety of potted plants and art installations, reflecting the creative personality of the homeowner.

His leisurely walk through the middle-class neighbourhood gave him the appreciation of the diversity of architectural styles and the well-maintained properties. There was money close to Crystal Cove's central business district and that the residents took pride in their homes, creating a sense of belonging and community in this friendly and inviting part of town.

"There is a lot of money in this small village. Especially Shore Drive," thought Danny as he looked at his watch, saw the time, and turned back towards his car and the drive back to the hotel.

Shore Drive in Crystal Cove New South Wales, with its mixture of no-frills and posh retail stores, offered a harmonious blend of luxury shopping and coastal charm, and when you add the Seashell Café, well thought Danny, he was going to enjoy his stay and indulge in the finer things in life while savouring the beauty of the sea.

Chapter Nine – Antonia 'Toni' Webster

As Danny settled into his car for the short drive back to the Poplar Inn, he was relieved that he didn't need to rely on his GPS this time. The route had become familiar with only one drive, and he could navigate it easily. With the engine purring to life, he began his journey.

The streetlights of Crystal Cove were on unnecessarily, even though there was still plenty of daylight and the sun was setting down. "It would seem the council prioritised the safety of its affluent residents and tourists," thought Danny.

The glow of streetlights and storefronts established a cosy and welcoming ambiance as Danny drove towards the hotel. The distance to the inn was short, and the drive felt more like a pleasant formality than a challenging journey.

As he cruised along the familiar roads, his mind wandered. His thoughts settled on Toni, the chef at the Seashell Café. She had made quite an impression on him during his recent visit. Somehow, one sandwich does not make her into an extraordinary chef, but Danny could not help but think that her culinary skills were exceptional. There had to be something else to her skills. Toni made a simple sandwich that lingered in his memory.

Danny couldn't help but wonder also about Toni's background. Antonia's first name was from a Spanish or Italian background, but her surname was Webster, more Anglo Saxon. *"Does it matter?"* Danny asked himself in thought. *"Of course not,"* was his answer to himself. *"I guess I am simply curious. Well, remember that curiosity killed the cat."* He smiled to himself at that last remark.

In his mind, when he visualised Toni as a young Gina Lollobrigida, which is how stunning she is. Her smile melted him. *"like sugar in water,"* thought Danny, with a smile on his face.

Lost in thought, Danny continued his leisurely drive back to the Poplar Inn, looking forward to his return and the possibility of dining at the Seashell Café once more. The memories of the delightful meal and the vibrant personality of Toni made him expect another visit to the café, and he couldn't wait to explore more of the culinary delights she offered.

Chapter Ten – Interesting Dinner

Danny arrived at the Poplar Inn with a sense of anticipation. He was getting hungry and as he entered the lobby, the soft glow of chandeliers and the comforting aroma of freshly cut flowers greeted him.

At the front desk, Gerti welcomed him. She had a warm smile and the cheerful demeanour as when he checked in, which put Danny at ease. "Good evening, Danny," she greeted him. "How may I assist you today?"

"What time is dinner served?"

"Dinner is from 6:30 PM until 10 PM, Monday through Thursday and 6:00 PM until 11 PM Friday through Sunday.

Looking at his watch, Danny decides he had time to refreshen up. "How about a dinner reservation for 7:30 PM. Can you accommodate me on such short notice?"

"Of course. Not a problem. We will see you then."

"And, if possible, I'd like a quiet table with a pleasant view, if available."

Without missing a beat, Gerti smiled. "We have a lovely corner table by the window that will provide a beautiful view of the garden. Would that be acceptable?"
Danny expressed his delight. "That sounds perfect, thank you."

"We look forward to having you join us for dinner, Danny, at 7:30 PM. Is there anything else I can assist you with?"

Danny shook his head. "No, that's it for now. Thank you, Gerti."

With his dinner reservation made, Danny made his way to his room. As Danny went upstairs, vintage artwork filled the hotel's corridor, and he couldn't help but admire the rich history of the establishment. Entering his room for the first time, he found his room decorated with classic furnishings. It was both cosy and inviting and at the rear of the inn. Danny noticed that someone had delivered his luggage and placed it on the bed, waiting for him to unpack. He unpacked his luggage. And then went to the bathroom to take a quick shower. After the shower, Danny settled in and had a moment to enjoy the view of the well-maintained garden from his balcony. He could hear the distant ocean waves lapping the shoreline of Crystal Cove.

Just as he was about to relax and unwind, his mobile phone rang, and Danny sees the caller id: Hair Man. It was Albert. "Hey, Albert, what's up?"

Albert's voice sounded concerned. "Danny, I just wanted to check in on you. You know how these trips can be sometimes. How's everything going?"

Danny appreciated Albert's concern and reassured him, "Everything's going well, Albert. The hotel is lovely, and I just made a dinner reservation for 7:30 PM. I'll fill you in on the details of my ride up to Crystal Cove later. How are things on your end?"

Albert sounded relieved. "That's good to hear, Danny, cariño. Things are going smoothly here. I have so much to tell you, but I just wanted to make sure you arrived safely. That new car of yours is powerful, you know."

"Yes, it is Albert, but you know me. I do not speed. Listen, I have to get ready for dinner. Will you be up later tonight? I can call later, and you can catch me up on whatever you wanted to share. Is that OK?"

"Of course, darling. You know I would wait up all night for you, always."

"I bet you would if you did not have something up your sleeves. Speak later, brother?"

"Alright. Have a splendid dinner and let me know if you need anything."

"Thanks, Albert. I'll catch up with you later. Take care," Danny replied, ending the call.

After Albert's call, Danny made his way to the hotel's bar and dining area at precisely 7:30 PM, the time of his reservation. As he entered the elegant space, Allison, the host warmly greeted him, for the evening. She had a friendly smile and a professional demeanour.

"Good evening, you must be Mr Monk, our 730 PM reservation," Allison said. "Your table is ready. Right this way, please."

"Yes, I am. Please lead the way."

Danny followed Allison as she led him through the well-appointed dining area. His corner table offered a beautiful view of the garden, just as Gertie had promised him.

As he went toward his table, he couldn't help but observe the other diners in the restaurant, each bringing their own unique story and presence to the room.

First, there was a couple in their mid-twenties who sat at a table adorned with rose petals and candlelight. They exchanged loving glances and held hands, clearly on the first days of their honeymoon. Their joy and excitement were infectious as they toasted to their new life together.

Then there was an older couple, probably in their late sixties, ready to dine in quiet contentment. They had an air of comfort and familiarity, sharing stories and smiles over a bottle of wine. The years had deepened their connection, and their love was evident in their warm gazes at each other.

Thoughts came into Danny's mind after seeing the young and older couples. *"Don't go there, Danny, do not go there,"* he told himself.

A quick glance to his left, he saw a solitary man in his forties who sat with a glass of whiskey. He appeared lost in thought, his eyes occasionally glancing at his phone. His solitude seemed deliberate, and there was an air of introspection about him, as if he were planning a plan or sorts.

Close to him on a separate table was a woman in her mid-fifties who sat at a table by the window. Confidence, elegance and wealth emanated from her. She had so much jewellery on her that the light from the chandeliers appear to bounce off her. While reading a book, she sipped her wine and enjoyed her own company. There was a sense of self-assuredness in her presence.

Finally, there next to the table that Danny was being escorted by Allison to sit was an elderly man who appeared to be around seventy-five years of age, who sat alone. He had a demeanour of quiet dignity, with an unopened book on the table. His wrinkled hands clutched a glass of red wine, and he observed the room with sharp eyes.

The man wore a well-tailored, muted tweed jacket and slacks, indicative of his timeless sense of style. Danny noticed the book closer. It lay unopen to the side of the table. The book seemed more like a prop, but it could be just a loyal companion on the countless literary journeys it has been on.

Danny continued observing him. His hair was salt and pepper hair, slightly dishevelled but still exuding an air of sophistication, framed by a face etched with the lines of a life richly lived. With his thin-framed glasses perched on the bridge of his nose, he exuded an air of intellect and sophistication. The frames, delicate and unobtrusive, traced the contours of his face with precision. The lenses, clear and polished, revealed a keenness in his gaze, suggesting a mind constantly at work.

They framed his eyes like windows to a well-versed mind, giving him an intellectual allure that complemented his overall appearance. There was something to him, but Danny felt maybe his imagination was getting the best of him.

Danny noticed the patrons had drinks but no food, which if the restaurant opened at 6:30 PM, like Gertie told Danny, they should at least be eating their main. This puzzled Danny. It made no sense, but the patrons did not seem fazed.

As Danny gets closer to his seat, the elderly man grabbed his arm. "Are you sitting by yourself, young man? Would you care to sit and accompany an old man during his dinner and make it an interesting dinner?"

Danny stops and looks at the gentleman a little closer.

With elegance and poise, the gentleman sipped the wine, savouring its aroma and delicate taste. The soft, warm light in the room created a calm and content atmosphere, a wonderful setting for a dinner. An aroma emitted from him. A balance between freshness and warmth, like a carefully crafted combination of citrus, spices, woods that lingers.

Danny perceived this gentleman as a man who had a life well-lived and enjoyed many simple pleasures, such as conversation. His appearance was well-groomed, and it appeared that he used makeup, like foundation or concealer, to diminish age-related skin concerns, thus creating a polished look. It seems that Danny was not destined to dine alone, so he answered the elderly man: "I was sir, but now, if you will accept me, I will be more than happy to enjoy my dinner with you, Mr....?"

"Reynolds, Abraham Reynolds Mr Monk."

"Please call me Danny."

"You can call me Abe, then, please sit. What are you drinking?"

"What are you having, Abe?"

"Allison recommended a nice glass of wine from the Brown Brothers vineyards with the unusual name brand of Patricia, a Shiraz, she said it was expensive, so I said yes, and the flavour had been wonderful It had a noticeably textural mouthfeel with bold, complex flavours. I love the deeply coloured tone of this drop."

"In that case, I will order us a bottle," and Danny waved to Allison, who came over and took Danny's order.

"Oh, my. Danny, it seems I am in for a long night of drink."

Danny smiled and just nods.

"So where is the food, Abe? I noticed everyone has a drink, but no food."

"Well, it seems....," and Abe got interrupted by a voice from the kitchen door.

"May I have your attention please, ladies and gentlemen?"

Danny turns and who turns out to be standing on the kitchen door?

No other than Antonia Webster. *"Oh yes, this is going to be an interesting dinner,"* thought Danny.

Chapter Eleven – Making Friends

Standing near the kitchen door is Toni, and she looked like she was about to give a speech.

"Ladies and gentlemen, I apologise for the delay in your evening meal. No excuse will express how disappointed I am in my failure to you with this delay. I hope you allow me to make it up to you. Tonight's meal, drinks, and dessert will be on me, and I am preparing a special dessert as we speak to make the evening worth your wait. Your elected meal will be out shortly and once again, I sincerely apologise."

As Toni turns to go back into the kitchen, she sees Danny and gives him a big smile, which he returned.

Abe looks at Danny and, smiled, asked: "You know her, Danny?"

"Well, yes, and no. I met her today at the café on Shore Drive when I went in for a quick lunch. I did not know she was the chef here at the inn."

"You are in for a massive surprise, young man. She is a wonderful chef. I been here now for over a week and dinner time is always to die for. Her specials are just wonderful. Her specialities are fish, seafood and lamb. Tonight, I ordered an entrée of delicate canapés featuring thinly sliced, velvety smoked salmon elegantly arranged on crisp, golden-brown Crostini complemented by a dollop of creamy dill-infused Creme Fraiche. For my main, I had a choice of a stunning chilled seafood platter adorned with a selection of Alaskan king crab legs, succulent lobster tails and plump Australian King prawns surround a mound of briny oysters on a bed of crushed ice and served with tangy cocktail sauce, mignonette and lemon wedges. I did not think I would have room for anything else after that. I believe I will savour the ocean's bounty with this meal."

"That sounds just superb," said Danny, looking at the menu. "I think I will do the canapés as well but go for the pan-seared Chilean sea bass. The menu says they will be cooked in such a manner to achieve a crispy, golden-brown exterior while maintaining a moist and flaky interior. It comes on a bed of sautéed spinach and roasted garlic mashed potatoes, drizzled with a velvety lemon beurre blanc sauce. Sounds just delightful, filling but not heavy."

Just as Danny puts the menu down, a young server comes out of the kitchen and comes toward their table.

"Mr Reynolds, your canapés. Chef added a few extra because of the wait."

A smiling Abe looked at the young man and mouthed a big thank you. The server turns to Danny: "And what may I get your sir? Sorry for the delay," he said with a sincere voice.

"I believe the canapés are too good to pass up and, for my main, I will go with the pan-seared Chilean sea bass."

"Excellent, sir. I will let the chef know your choice and bring it right up," and he departs to place the order.

"Dig in, Abe, please do not wait for me."

"Are you sure? It looks impolite."

"No, please dig in into your canapés."

"Tell you what Danny, let's share and when yours comes out, I will pick a few from your order. How about that?"

"You got yourself a deal, Abe," Danny said as he reached for one of the canapés.

Slowly, another young waiter came out of the kitchen and headed to the table with the young couple. Danny could not see what the plates held, but it looked lovely.

Then the server that came to Danny's and Abe's table came out with two plates and headed toward the table of the older couple. and the lady seemed to clap when she saw her plate.

As the second server went back to the kitchen, the first server came out with a single plate and delivered it to the elegant lady in her fifties who looked at the plate being served in front of her but kept reading her book as if uninterested in the food and not even acknowledging the server. The server pulled away from the table and the lady put her book down and immediately started eating. "Wealth does not bring class with it," thought Danny, watching her response.

Abe notices the same reaction and Danny's face and makes a quick comment.

"You noticed how she reacted? Well, that is Ms Lititz Carter, a widower. She lives in Toorak Victoria and according to her: 'I just love travelling through the little towns of New South Wales', Abe mimics making air quotes. According to what she said, or what I overheard, she is quite wealthy, but I'm not sure. She has chosen to stay in the Coral Cove Room.

Finally, Allison comes out of the kitchen with one more plate and delivers it to the whiskey man, who nods and starts devouring his order.

"Well, it looks like the last one will be you, Danny," said Abe.

"I was the last one to arrive, but I am sharing your canapés so I'm not doing too bad and now everyone seems a bit more relax with food on their table."

"They are all an interesting lot, this mob," added Abe.

"Really? How so Abe?"

"Have you met any of them?"

"Not really Abe. Just you. Why?"

Abe looks around as if to make sure no one is listening in and smiled he said to Danny: "Well, the young couple they go by Jim and Sally Wentworth. What you may have discerned from their amorous actions is that they are here on their honeymoon."

"Yes, I gather that by their body signals Abe. Amazingly easy to pick up," Danny replied with a mischievous smile himself.

"What you do not know, Danny, is that since their arrival, Robert is going into their room when they retire for the evening."

"Who is Robert?" Danny asked.

"The young porter. He takes people's baggage to their rooms and helps around the place."

A smiled Abe just nods his head toward the young couple and continued: "The young couple are taking part in a ménage à trois from the sounds I hear from across the hall. I am right across from them, you know. They are in the Mermaid's Retreat, which is a charming hideaway for those seeking a romantic escape. It has a balcony, so they can enjoy the ocean breezes and they leave the balcony doors open. Sound travels out both their front door and the balcony door. I am across the hall from them in the more modest Nautical Nook, looking onto Shore Drive. I try to stay within my budget when I travel, you know what I mean?"

"Yes, I understand, Abe, keeping to a budget is always important in all aspects of life. Wow, that is something else. They look so happy."

"They are probably thrilled, but you never know what makes people tick, do you?" as he places a canapé into his mouth and closes his eyes as if he is in ecstasy.

After enjoying the canapé, Abe points in his left index finger at the older couple.

"Now there we have Mr Aloysius and Mrs Evelyn Maxwell from Mosman. They are staying in the Sea Breeze suite and checked in after they came to visit a grandson in Byron Bay nearby. Got into a quarrel with him, and he threw them out, so here they are licking their wounds, so to speak. I hear he is a banker in one of the big four banks, not sure which one. He looks like a banker, does he not?"

Danny looked at the Maxwells' and turned to Abe. "Abe, I am not sure what a banker is supposed to look like. He seems like everyone else."

Scoffing, Abe simply said: "Oh, yes my young friend, he is a banker. I can tell," as he points to his own nose with his finger.

"Danny, do you mind if I have the last canapé?" as he reaches to the platter.

"Go right ahead," said Danny as he sees a young man in a chef's uniform coming his way with his canapé platter. "There are more coming as we speak."

The young chef places the platter on the table.

"With compliments of Chef Toni, Mr Monk."

"Thank you very much young man. What is your name?"

"My name is Marcus Aurelius Burton, sir, a pleasure to meet you."

"I presume you work with Chef Toni?"

"Yes, I am finishing up my apprenticeship with her."

"I heard from Mr Reynolds here that Chef Toni is quite a chef?"

"She is awesome. I have learned so much and she has said she believes I am ready to go solo soon. I cannot wait."

"That is good to hear. Give her my thanks for the canapés."

"Oh, I will. Would you like allusion to bring you another bottle of wine?"

Danny looks at Abe who just smiles and Danny nods to Marcus who in turn takes the empty bottle and motions Allison to bring another one.

As Marcus moves away, Abe grabs another canapé and said: "Thanks for the next bottle of wine. It is quite divine. A lot out of my league, so I'm enjoying it heaps."

"Please do Abe. I got you covered tonight on the wine."

"But I thought the chef was paying tonight?" stated Abe.

Danny smiles. "That is what she said, but I will not let her pay for ours. Let me handle it. Now tell me what you know about the lonesome gentleman," Danny leans his head towards the man sitting by himself with the whiskey, hoped Abe can also identify him.

"Oh, that is Mr Homer Witham. I think he is in the Lighthouse Loft. I read about him in the Sydney Financial Times. You heard what he did, right?"

"No Abe I have not. What did he do?"

"He defrauded over $30 million dollars in crypto funds from his investors. I heard something connected him to organised crime as well. He is out on bail before going to trial in December. Quite a nasty sort of fellow. You might want to stir clear of him."

Looking at the man, Danny did not sense a threat from him, but appearances can be deceiving. Just then, Allison shows up with their evening meals.

"Mr Reynolds, your order, as you requested, with extra

lemons. Mr Monk, your sea bass," as she places the plate in front of Danny, Allison added: "Compliment of Chef Webster. She said she hopes you enjoy it but to make sure you leave room for dessert."

Danny smiled and just responds to Allison, stating: "Please let her know I will indeed leave room for her dessert."

Allison smiled back at both Abe and Danny and rushes into the kitchen to relay the message.

Abe takes another bite from his lobster tail and looked at Danny and said: "Young man, you make friends quickly."

Danny ponders that statement for a few seconds and can only said to Abe: "I guess I do, Abe. I guess I do."

Chapter Twelve – Ride Home

The rest of the evening went pleasantly for Danny and his new companion, Abe, as they chatted and got to learn a bit about themselves.

"So, Abe, are you still working or are you retired from the rat race?" asked Danny.

"Goodness, I have not heard work being mentioned in those terms in a while. Yes, I am retired. Now, for over fifteen years."

"What did you do for a living, Abe?"

"I was involved in two businesses at the same time in my younger years. First there was Nullica Security Service providing your normal residential security services to people's homes, you know, camera, alarms, that sort of thing. One thing led to another and a few years later, I took over Nullica Locks and Safes when the owner had a heart attack and the family needed to sell in a hurry. I got it for a bargain and, since it complimented my security business, it worked out great for me. I grew the business over the years and later sold the business to the American security service ADT as they started getting into the business in Australia. For the past fifteen years, I was commuting."

"Commuting?"

"Well, let me clarify. I dislike winter. Makes me wear too many clothes, so I spend six months in Australia, September through March, and I then spend the next six months in warmer climates around the world enjoying their spring and summer. Frankly, I own no winter clothes, and it gives me time for my favourite hobby, bird watching in parks and national parks." added Abe with a chuckle.

"Now that is quite a life, Abe. Selling your business must have been profitable to you if you do not mind me saying."

"Not at all Danny. Yes, the sale price was substantial but there were new investments and wise acquisitions that I made during my travels which added to my net worth, and I get to spend my time in lovely places like the Poplar Inn in beautiful Crystal Cove and make new friends," Abe said pointing to Danny.

"I bow to your wisdom, Abe and good taste in friends."

Abe laughed at Danny's remark and asked: "How about you, Danny? Are you retired?"

Danny went to explain his business and Abe listen intensely, sipping his glass of wine, and nodding and asked the occasional question. Danny did not detail any of his own investments nor acquisitions with Albert and for sure did not mention Alessia but concentrated on his bookstore and other legitimate business ventures with Albert and just stated that he was taking time off to relax and gather his thoughts.

"Gentlemen, pardon my interruption. Are you ready for dessert?" asked the young server.

Abe and Danny looked at each other and Abe indicates he was not having dessert, but Danny was ready.

"My friend, Mr Reynolds, is not having any, but I am ready for dessert. By the way, what is your name?"

"It is Frankie. Frankie Lemmon sir."

"Nice to meet you, Frankie. I am going to be staying here at the inn for a couple of weeks, so I thought we could be on a first name basis. Call me Danny."

Frankie was a bit surprised at Danny's gesture but carefully answered back. "OK Danny. I will bring you the dessert in a minute."

"Well, it seems you continue to make friends, or at least are trying to do so."

"I am not a very formal person, Abe. I hate the Mrs and the Mr in front of names all the time. To start yes, but once I get to know someone, it is first name basis for me.

"I understand Danny. Frankie is a nice boy. I am told he has been working here for over two years and has a very reputable disposition and is quite liked by the guests."

"While I wait for dessert, can I order you a coffee, Abe?"

"Oh, no Danny, I will not sleep tonight if I have a coffee this late."

Danny looked at his watch. It was close to 10 PM. The evening had flown, and he had a marvellous time with Abe. Time simply flew by in delightful conversation.

Frankie returns holding Danny's dessert and places it in front of Danny and looking at Abe, as a temptation, describes to Danny what he has delivered.

"Chef tonight has created a special dessert to make up for the lateness of the dinner. It is a lemon-lavender panna cotta served with a luscious berry compote. The smooth and creamy panna cotta has a delicate infusion of citrus and floral notes, perfectly complemented by the burst of flavour from the mixed berry compote which chef recommends a Harvey Bristol Cream sherry as a complement."

"It looks wonderful, Danny, but I am full. Please dig in and if you do not mind, I will retire in the evening. I had a wonderful time. You stay and finish your dessert." Abe gets up and looks around the restaurant and then states: "Well, it looks you are closing up shop as well. You are the last one. See you later, Danny."

"See you around, Abe," said Danny as he takes his fork to start on the panna cotta and told Frankie to bring him a glass of Harvey Bristol Cream sherry to wash the dessert down.

The dessert is erupting with flavour as he bites into it and then, out of the corner of his eye, Danny sees Toni coming out of the kitchen with a glass in her hand.

"You ordered a sherry, sir?"

Danny quickly stands and, with a dumb grin on his face, he can only respond: "Yes, I did. Would you care to join me in a sherry as well? The panna cotta is marvellous, by the way."

"And so, it should. I made it tonight and yes, I will join you," and Toni motions to Frankie to bring her a sherry as well.

As Danny sits down, Toni's exquisite looks still captivated him. Working in a kitchen has to be exhausting, but Toni just looks so refreshed, sitting there with him. Frankie quickly returns with a glass of sherry.

"Thanks, Frankie. Please help Milo start the cleanup process. You think you can help him out?"

"Yes chef. You take it easy. I got it," and he hurried off into the kitchen.

Watching Frankie go through the kitchen door, Danny addresses Toni: "Dinner was just spectacular Toni. I am quite impressed with your culinary skills. Where did you train and learn these skills?

"I was fortunate to have two marvellous teachers and mentors. The first one you met already, my mother Cecilia, and the second one was Auguste Ducharme at the Gualtiero Marchesi's Gourmet Cookery School in L'Albereta, Italy, where

I spent my final years learning more. I am glad you approve of both," Toni said with a slight giggled as she sipped her sherry.

"A French master chef teaching at a top-notch Italian culinary school. That has to be interesting, to say the least," said Danny.

"Interesting was probably one word I would not have used to describe my tutelage, but it was indeed quite instructive, and I appreciated everything I learned there."

The banter went back and forth and before Danny realised, it was midnight and Toni got up and said her goodnight and started walking back to the kitchen.

"How are you getting home?" Danny asked.

"I usually hitch a ride with Frankie. He should be done by now in the kitchen."

"Why don't you let him allow me to take you home, if I may?"

Toni takes a few moments to consider the proposition and gives Danny a big smile. "OK, you got yourself a passenger. You do not mind?"

"Not at all. I just want to spend as much time as I can tonight with you, so this is my clumsy attempt at more time with you."

Toni laughed aloud and smiled at Danny.

"Well, it is working. Wait for me in the lobby."

Danny watched her walk into the kitchen and took his last sip of his sherry and went to Allison, who was the last employee left in the room.

"allusion, I do not want chef webster to pay for Mr Reynolds nor my dinner tonight. Please put those meals and drinks in my room. OK?"

"Of course, Mr Monk," as you wish. "Have a good evening."

Danny goes into the lobby and stands waiting for Toni, and he felt all giddy.

"Why am I feeling this way?" he thought to himself and then he hears footsteps and sees Robert, the porter, coming down the stairs.

"Good evening Mr Monk," he said.

"Good evening," responded Danny, and watched Robert walk past him in a hurry. and could smell a woman's scent on him.

"I guess it was a good evening for you as well," Danny thought.

"I'm ready Danny."

Danny turned and saw Toni.

"Wow, I did not recognise you with clothes on."

"What?" a startled Toni said.

"Oh, wait Toni, that did not come out right. I meant I did not recognise you without your chef's uniform."

Toni relaxed a bit and smiled.

"For a moment, I thought you were some sort of deviant, Danny."

Surprised by her remark, Danny only answered with: "No, I am not."

"Shame."

"What? Was Danny's remark.

Toni laughed aloud and placed her arm into his.

"Lead me to your chariot, Danny."

"Beautiful, smart, and with a sense of humour and can cook on top of that. I need to be careful with this one," thought Danny as he takes Toni out the front door of the inn.

Chapter Thirteen – The Captain and the First Mate

Danny escorts Toni out of the inn towards his car. Even under the moonlight Toni can see that Danny has an expensive taste in cars and makes a little remark: "My, oh, my Danny, you must have dropped a few cents in this beauty."

Opening the door for Toni, all Danny can say is: "You know Toni, you are the second person who has made the same statement."

Starting the car, Toni gives Danny her address, and he keys the address into the car's GPS system. After a few minutes Toni places her hand on Danny's right arm and asks Danny to change direction towards a nearby lake. Surprised a bit by the request, Danny simply nods, and he followed her directions after he turned the GPS off.

They arrived at a nearby lake and found themselves surrounded by a serene stillness that only a moonlit night at the lake could provide.

"I did not know this lake was here. Does it have a name? Danny asks.

"The locals call it Crystal Cove Lake, but it shows up on the maps as Whispering Pines Lake. Not sure why?"

Danny looks around and sees the water's surface reflected the shimmering stars above, creating an enchanting atmosphere. Toni's spontaneous decision to detour to the lake caught Danny by surprise, but he couldn't deny the allure of the peaceful scene.

They parked the car near the water's edge, and the soft sound of crickets filled the air. Toni turned to Danny with a mischievous glint in her eyes and said, "You know, sometimes you just need a break from the routine, Danny. Life's too short to always follow the planned path."

Danny grinned, intrigued by Toni's adventurous spirit. "You're absolutely right. What did you have in mind?"

Toni pointed towards a small rowboat moored nearby. "How about a midnight row on the lake? It's been ages since I've done something spontaneous like this. You can row and be captain and I'll be first mate."

Danny hesitated for a moment, then went along with the impromptu plan. They climbed into the boat, the creaking of the wood beneath them adding to the night's mysterious ambiance. Danny took the oars, and they glided over the calm water, the only sounds being the gentle lapping of the lake against the boat and the distant calls of nocturnal creatures.

As Danny rowed, Toni shared stories from her past, anecdotes that made them laugh and moments that made them reflect. The moonlight danced on the water, casting a magical glow around them. It felt like they were in a world of their own, far removed from the hustle and bustle of their everyday lives.

"I was blabbing about me. Now it is your turn, Danny. Tell me about you."

Danny returned the request going over his life in Northport. He shared his father had worked at a local hardware store Williamson's and his mother had been a at the Northport Library on Mavis Street. He explained that after he finished high school, his initial career goal was to get into architecture. Danny explained that he quickly realised that after taking the first course that he was not an architect at heart. Instead, he found out that he enjoyed the retail world.

To help with the expenses of going to the university, he told Toni how his mother contacted Mr. Hebert McCullum, owner of *McCullum Booksellers*, and how he got hired as a part-time retail salesperson, shelf stocker and general all-rounder.

Finally, he explained that this was a great decision for him and when old man McCullum was ready to retire, Danny took all his inheritance, got a bank loan, and purchased the store and its inventory and added the collection of books his parents had acquired over the years.

"That is how *Village Books & Stuff* came into existence. Over the years, some acquisitions, and wise investments and new partnerships with some talented entrepreneurs were good to me and here I am sitting in a rowboat in the middle of this lake telling you my life's story."

Toni laughed at how he concluded his story, and Danny smiled at her. *"She looks beautiful in the moonlight,"* thought Danny.

After a while, Toni suggested they anchor the boat in a quiet spot. They lay back, gazing up at the star-studded sky, lost in a comfortable silence. The air was crisp, and a gentle breeze carried the scent of pine trees from the surrounding woods.

"Smell the scent of pine trees, Toni?"

Toni took a deep breath and answered: "Now I see why it is called Whispering Pines lake," and she smiled at Danny.

As they lay side by side, the closeness between them grew. Toni turned her head to look at Danny, her eyes sparkling in the moonlight. "You know," she said, "sometimes it's good to escape the ordinary and just be in the moment."

Danny nodded in agreement, and he looked at his watch and saw the time.

"Toni, do you know what time it is?"

Toni looked at her own watch and saw the time: 5:17 AM. "Well, Captain Danny, you make time simply so marvellous that it just flew. I am glad we have spent this time together here, on this lake, enjoying the evening."

Danny looked at Toni with a big grin and simply said: "I agree first, mate."

As the first light of dawn painted the horizon, they rowed back to shore, carrying with them the magic of a night spent under the stars.

"Let's get you home now. I am sure your mother will be worried."

Toni lets a big laugh out: "I do not live with my mother, Danny. I am not a child. I got my own place so get that GPS online again and let me fix you breakfast at my place."

Danny reset the GPS and in twenty minutes, the automated voice of the GPS announced they had arrived.

Toni's house was a changed Queenslander style home.

The typical Queenslander house is a distinctive style found in the northeastern part of Australia, known for its raised design to combat the region's hot climate. Toni's home was a little different.

Just like the typical Queenslander, Toni's home was a two-storey house with wraparound verandas that provide shade and a cool outdoor living space. Ornate timber posts supported these verandas, featuring intricate detailing like decorative brackets, or turned balusters. Constructed using timber, the home showcases the warm, natural tones of the material. The exterior was painted in classic colours, white, and a light cream, which Danny could even distinguish in the early morning sun light.

Similar to all Queenslanders, the house featured a steep, high-pitched roof made of corrugated metal, with some gables and dormer windows incorporated, which added further architectural interest to the roofline.

The home had the typical large French doors which opened onto the verandas, allowing for ample natural light and ventilation. Sash windows with timber framing added more of the classic touch to the home's facade.

Finally, what Queenslander home does not have lush tropical gardens with vibrant flowers, palms and other greenery. These gardens complement the natural beauty of the Queenslander design and add to the overall tropical ambiance.

"Toni, I know we are in New South Wales, but you have brought a harmonious combination of practicality, ornate detailing and a connection to the surrounding landscape to your home that is both functional and aesthetically pleasing. I am impressed. Did you design it?"

"Goodness no. I hired someone to do the exterior and a professional landscaper to do the garden. An interior designer helped me with some of the inside. Come on, let me fix you breakfast."

Danny gets out of the car and goes around to open Toni's car door and walks to her front door. As Danny stood in Toni's doorway, her inviting smile, and the prospect of the aroma of freshly brewed coffee and sizzling bacon wafting from her kitchen tempted him. However, an unexpected wave of uncertainty held him back. They had shared an adventurous night by the lake, and although a connection had sparked between them, the daylight brought with it the weight of the real world. Danny couldn't shake off the thought that maybe this was just a fleeting moment, a spontaneous escapade meant to stay within the confines of that magical night.

Danny did not want to move too fast after the debacle with Alessia. He pondered the implications of accepting Toni's invitation for breakfast. Would it signal a commitment from Toni? Or was it merely a friendly gesture? The prospect of facing the morning light and the reality beyond the enchanting night made him hesitate, his mind grappling with the balance between the desire to extend their connection and the fear of potentially complicating a beautiful, albeit brief, moment in time. In that moment of hesitation, Danny's thoughts raced, unsure of whether stepping into Toni's kitchen meant stepping into something more profound or risking the delicacy of the memories they had just created. He went slowly.

"Toni, I am going to pass on breakfast but would love a raincheck. I am tired from the ride here from Northport. Do you mind?"

Toni's radiant smile faltered ever so slightly when Danny hesitated at the doorway, his response more measured than she expected. She had envisioned a continuation of the night's spontaneity, an extension of the connection they had forged by the lake. However, when Danny asked for a raincheck on breakfast, Toni's eyes flickered with a mix of surprise and mild disappointment.

In that moment, Toni questioned if perhaps she had misread the situation. Had her invitation, which seemed like a casual and friendly gesture to her, come across differently to Danny? Her mind raced to analyse the night's events, wondering if she had unintentionally rushed things or misinterpreted the depth of their connection. Toni, known for her open and carefree nature, reassessed whether she had inadvertently created an expectation that Danny wasn't prepared to meet. The ambiguity hung in the air as she processed his response, trying to decipher whether it was a matter of timing or a sign of hesitance on Danny's part.

"Of course, Danny, I understand. A raincheck it is."

As she gracefully accepted his raincheck, Toni masked her internal questions with a reassuring smile, respecting the boundaries Danny may have needed to establish.

At that moment Toni placed her key into the door and gently closes the door on Danny mouthing a soft 'good night' and Dany walked back to the car.

In that moment, the bridge between their worlds seemed to shift, leaving room for a more deliberate exploration of what lay ahead. Little did they know that this moment would mark the beginning of a new chapter in their lives.

Chapter Fourteen – Home Whitham

The shrill ringtone pierced through the air, causing a momentary disruption in the slumber of Danny's sleep. He swiftly reached for his mobile phone, the source of the intrusive sound. As he glanced at the screen, the bright display revealed the time: 11:40 AM. However, what caught his attention more was the caller ID that read "Hair Man."

Danny answered the call. He never knew what to expect when Albert called. He answered the call in a calm and collected voice: "Hi Albert. I know why you are calling. Do not panic."

On the other end of the line, Albert's voice trembled with hysteria. His words rushed out frantically, filled with urgency and anxiety. The contrast between Danny's composed assurance and Albert's distressed state created a tense atmosphere.

"Danny, sweetness, you did not call me. I thought something terrible had happened to you. Are you OK?"

Danny maintained his calm demeanour, ready to address whatever situation had prompted Albert's frantic call.

"Albert, I am so sorry I just forgot to call you back, and I had a wonderful evening, but late at night, and I was still asleep when you rang."

"Asleep at almost noon? Danny, are you alone?"

"Yes, Albert, I am alone. Who do you think I am?"

"Oh, I know who you are, Danny. That is why I asked the question. Tell me, tell me everything. What happened last night that has made you so late in calling your best friend in the entire world?"

Danny thought about this. If he answered Albert's question, he would be on the phone for an hour or more and he was now getting hungry, so he decided that he would have to postpone his old friend once more.

"Albert, look, I have not had breakfast and I am hungry. Let me let you grab some food and I promise I will call you back."

"Danny, if you cannot call me, I am grabbing my 1998 Bentley Mulsanne and roar into Crystal Cove to find you."

"Albert, I promise I will not fail you. Now let me hang up and I will call you after I finish getting some food.

"OK, darling, I will wait for your call. We need to talk for it has been a few weeks since you left, OK? Ciao!"

Danny quickly gets up, shaves, showers, dresses, and goes out his front door to grab some food.

As he does, he notices Abe going into the Sea Breeze Suite. *"I thought Abe was in the Nautical Nook room,"* thought Danny.

"Good morning Abe."

A startled Abe turns around and quickly responded to Danny.

"Oh, hi Danny. I thought you were out and about already."

"Why are you going into the Sea Breeze Suite? I thought you were staying in the Nautical Nook room, or did I hear you wrong the other night?"

Looking a bit embarrassed, Abe smiled and just said: "I guess I am getting old, Danny. Cannot seem to remember which way I am going." He looks at the nameplate on the door: Sea Breeze Suite, and points to it.

"Now, how could I have been so wrong? I am glad you stop me. There's a chance that I could have broken the door lock or something. In the future, I must be more careful about my surroundings. Thanks Danny," and he heads toward his own room, pointing out the name plates of the other rooms on the floor as he gets to his room.

Abe inserts his key in, opens the door, smiles at Danny, and gives a wave, and closes the door behind him.

Danny walked toward the stairs and makes a second mental note of the floor plan. When you come up the stairs on the right is the Coral Cove Room which is occupied by Ms Lititz Carter, then the Nautical Nook, Abe's room and then the Sea Breeze Suite which Mr Aloysius and Mrs Evelyn Maxwell share.

On the left is Mr Homer Witham's in the Lighthouse Loft. The Driftwood Den was next to it, and Danny was unsure if it was occupied or not. After that is the Mermaid's Retreat, where Jim and Sally Wentworth are staying.

Finally, at the end of the hall is the Captain's Quarters, Danny's suite.

Standing at the top of the stairs, Danny wonders how Abe could have confused the rooms, for they are clearly marked, and he did not seem senile during his evening conversation the other night. *"Maybe just a mental lapse,"* Danny thought, and he continued downstairs to the restaurant.

As Danny arrived at the restaurant, Gertie greeted him: "Hi Danny, ready for lunch?"

"Actually, Gertie, is it too late for breakfast? I seemed to have slept through it."

"We usually do not do that, but we are an accommodating lot, and I am sure Samuel will round up some breakfast for you. Please follow me," as Gertie takes Danny to a table by the window.

As they walk in, Danny notices that only two other tables have customers seated. One by Mr Aloysius and Mrs Evelyn

Maxwell and next to them is Mr Homer Witham, who is carrying a conversation with them. Seeing Danny come in, they all stop their conversation, smiled at Danny as he passed by, and then continue in their talk, but in a much softer tone.

"Is this table OK for you, Danny?"

"Yes, of course. It is fine. It is a perfect spot."

"So, what breakfast can I get Samuel to get for you?"

It did not take Danny long to answered, for he knew what he wanted.

"Do I dare ask for French toast with maple syrup, butter and a strong cappuccino?"

"Is that it?"

"Yes, why? Am I asking for too much? Asked Danny.

"Of course not. I was thinking you were going to ask for something really exotic for breakfast, like friend squid."

Danny makes a funny face and just had to asked.

"Has anyone actually asked for that? Fried squid?"

"Well, no, but once we had a Thai couple once ask us for mango leaves filled with rice, fish paste and fried beetles for breakfast, so now we are ready for any surprise. French toast with maple syrup and butter and a strong cappuccino coming right up."

As Gertie went to the kitchen to place his order, a notion came to Danny.

In his conversation with Abe last night, he remembers Abe saying that his room was across from Jim and Sally Wentworth, but it is not. Abe's room is up toward Danny's. Abe's room is across the Driftwood Den. There is no way Abe could hear Jim and Sally Wentworth's escapades with Robert unless he was listing in by the door.

Danny thought he should ask Gertie when she returns if the Driftwood Den was empty or reserved for someone else. Just then, he gets a tap on his shoulder, and he turns to see Mr Homer Witham standing next to him.

"Hi there. My name is Mr Homer Witham. Mind if I sit with you for a moment?"

"Of course, please sit, Mr Witham. My name is Danny Monk. Mostly I go by Danny."

"A pleasure Danny. Please call me Homer. I noticed last night you had a conversation with the old guy, Reynolds. Right, I think that is his name."

"Yes, he grabbed my arms and asked me to have dinner with him. Pleasant chap."

"Reynolds seems to ask a lot of questions. Did he seem super interested in your business, Danny?"

That was an interesting question Witham asked, and Danny took a few seconds to think of his answer as he recalled his conversation with Abe last night.

"Mr Reynolds went over a little of his history and then asked me to share mine, which I did. I saw no harm in doing so. Why do you ask?"

Witham sits back and seems to think about how to phrase his answer to Danny.

"That is why I was speaking with the Maxwells. Reynolds had corralled them in the last few days, just like he did me, and asked a lot of questions about investments, portfolio size, current asset allocation, mix of equities, fixed income, and some alternative investments. Reynolds asked if they were comfortable with their overall risk tolerance. I am surprised he did not do the same with you."

"Well, he told me he lives of his investments and acquisitions, so maybe he was just trying to learn on how to improve his returns. Does not seem harmful, does it?"

"Maybe, maybe not. It was not such much the conversation, but things around the conversation?"

"What do you mean, Whitham?"

"Reynolds would ask if I had valuable jewellery. He asked the same of the Maxwells? What does that have to do with investments? Did he ask you that question?"

Danny was getting a bit frustrated with Whitham, so he asked him a direct question. "Homer, what do you do for a living?"

That question took Whitham aback, and it took him a few seconds to compose himself and answer Danny.

"I am retired. In the past, my job was as a CCT."

"I'm unfamiliar with what a CCT is. What does it stand for?"

"It means a certified cryptocurrency trader. I worked in the cryptocurrency markets until last year."

"I do not know a lot about cryptocurrency trading. What are the basics of it? Can you provide me with a simple answer that as a layperson I would understand?"

Witham looks at Danny as if to said why you need to know this, but relented and gives him a quick explanation: "Basically this currency makes money. There are three basic strategies. First one is to invest or trade, similar to stock market investments. For example, when trading in cryptocurrency, you start a long position by purchasing an asset, hoping its price will rise, similar to stock market investments. Somewhere between those two points, you make money. Second one is to stake and lend. That means you use your coins to stake or lend to others. Finally, you can mine or earn rewards within the blockchain system."

"Money? Like in real money?"

"Yes."

"And was Reynolds asking you about that?"

"No, he kept asking me if I had invested in such things like gold chains, gold watches, diamonds rings. Stuff like that. The same with the Maxwells."

"How did Mr and Mrs Maxwell react to Reynolds' questions?"

"They were apprehensive after a while. At first everything seems like a normal conversation, but Reynolds kept making points of Mrs Maxwell's necklace, for example, and Mr Maxwell's watch. Really, a strange course in the conversation. They basically cut him off and he went away to his own table and then you came in last night and he grabbed you to sit with him, so they thought he was going after you with his questions."

Danny thought about the conversation he had with Abe last night and again, he could only recollect a pleasant conversation. Abe didn't ask any of the questions Whitham was saying.

"I am not sure what to say, Homer. Abe just did not ask me any of these questions, nor did we discuss investments."

Whitham looked at Danny and just stood up and said: "Just keep an eye on him. He is not what he seems to be. I feel it."

Danny does not know why he defended Abe at that moment but answered Whitham with a sharp response: "None of us are who we seem to project, Homer. We all wear masks of some type."

Whitham just nodded to Danny and walked out of the restaurant just as Gertie was bringing Danny his breakfast.

"He seemed to have left in a huff. Is everything OK? Was he not happy with his lunch?"

"I am sure everything is fine, Gertie. Mr Whitham was just curious about a few things and apparently was not happy with my answers."

"Well never mind him. Enjoy your breakfast."

"I will. The French toast looks fantastic, and the coffee was divine."

"See, I told you Samuel would take care of you."

"You did Gertie. You did indeed."

Chapter Fifteen – Lititz Carter

After finishing the sumptuous breakfast prepared by Samuel, Danny returned to his room to get ready for the rest of the day. He had not made plans with Toni, and after that awkward moment on her doorstep, Danny was not sure if she still wanted to see him. After Danny freshened up, he returned downstairs and went to ask Gertie if there was any information, brochures, etc., that he could pick up and see if there was something for him to do for the rest of the day.

As he arrives at the reception desk, Gertie is helping the widow. Ms Lititz Carter and Danny cannot help but overhear the conversation.

"I tell you Mrs Bailey, I think someone went through my room and it was not the cleaning staff," Ms Lititz Carter stated.

"Ms Lititz Carter, other than Robert and the rest of the cleaning crew, no one may go into a guest's room without permission. Was there something missing? Was the room dishevelled in any way?"

"No, it was not. I felt a presence in the room as if someone who was not supposed to be there came in and roamed around the room, touching things but carefully making sure they were placed as he found them."

"You said 'he', so you saw him?"

"No Mrs Bailey, it just felt like a male. An evil male at that. I am sure you caught him on camera as he entered my room."

"We only have security cameras outside the inn, Ms Carter, not inside the inn and not in the hallway leading to the room."

"Well, I am not sure what I am feeling, but I sensed someone, and I am seldom wrong about my feelings, Mrs Bailey."

"I will tell Samuel your concern and I will ask him to double make sure the door to your room is secured."

"I am surprised that you still have keys to the rooms and not the electronic locks most places have, but I guess it would take away from the charm of the inn," Ms Carter said.

Gertie just smiled and did not respond but rather assumed the conversation was over with Ms carter and directed her glance and question to me.

"Mr Monk, how can I help you?"

Ms Carter turned around and gave Danny a quick look over as if checking him as the potential intruder into her room, but satisfied that Danny seemed harmless, she just smiled at him as she stepped away from the reception desk heading out the front door.

"Gertie, is everything alright?"

"Not a problem, Danny. We cannot handle. Ms Carter seems to think someone was in her room but reported nothing missing, so all's good. How can I help you?"

"Just wondering if you have any suggestions for me on how to spend the rest of the day?"

Gertie turns her back to Danny and opens a counter door and reaches in and comes out with a brochure and hands it to Danny.

"Here Danny is a brochure of our nearest walking trail. It is very easy, rugged, so I recommend you wear your hiking shoes or boots because some of the ragged rocks will destroy runners along the trail. The trail leads to a wonderful outlook about four kilometres from the parking lot, and it is worth the effort."

"Oh, I did not bring any hiking shoes or boots. Anywhere in Crystal Cove, do you recommend?"

"No, we do not have any place here that would have those, but you can drive up to Byron Bay, which is only twenty minutes away. I think it is called Marty's Camping & Disposals. Been there for years. An excellent selection, I am told."

"Excellent. I think I will do just that." Placing the brochure into his back pocket, Danny said to Gertie: "Thanks for the brochure and the suggestion, Gertie."

"My pleasure Danny."

Gertie calls out to Danny as he is headed to the front door, "Are you not meeting with Toni today?"

Surprised at the statement, Danny returns to the reception desk.

"No, we had a lovely time last night, but we made no plans. I believe she is off work today and tomorrow. I thought she wanted time to, so I did not ask. May I ask how you knew we had spent time together, Gertie?"

"Small town Danny, small town."

Danny understood what Gertie meant by that statement.

Living in Northport, not much got past Albert, so why would it not be the same in Crystal Cove?

As Danny walked toward his car, he felt the midday sun stinging a little, so he decided not to bring the top down and, after consulting his GPS and punching the name of the hiking place, he headed towards Byron Bay.

The drive was uneventful, and the GPS was successful in locating the store. Danny parked and walked into the place and found it to be an interesting mix of modern and old disposal store.

As Danny stepped through the creaking wooden door, the scent of aged leather and freshly treated canvas welcomed him. The store seemed to be a haven for those seeking a nostalgic connection to the great outdoors. Wooden shelves, weathered and marked by time, proudly display an eclectic collection of classic camping equipment. A vintage stove, its polished surface, reflected the flickering light of the overhead lights, and Danny spotted several timeless enamelware mugs and retro-patterned sleeping bags reminiscent of a bygone era.

"Good afternoon, mate, my name is Jono, how may I help you?" said the acne faced young man.

"Hi Jono, I was told that this was the place to go to if I needed hiking boots. Can you help me?"

"Yeah. Doing some bushwalking? Will you be doing a bush bash? Will you be needing some gaiters?"

Danny only knew what bushwalking meant. The rest was new to him, so he reached in his back pocket and handed the kid the brochure and said: "This is where I am headed".

"Oh, you need some good gear there, mate. This trail name lulls you into a sense of complacency but it is hard and treacherous if you are not prepared. I do not know how it got the name Cloud Nine Express but I recommend you try on the Salomon's X Ultra 4 Mid GTX. An outstanding quality shoe. It will do just great on this trail. What's your size?"

Danny shares his shoe size and goes and sits down while the acne boy brings him the shoe to try on.

"Here you go, mate. It should fit you like a glove."

Danny takes the box from Jono and tries the shoe, and one foot feels good. Danny then tries the second foot and walks around the store and his feet feel like they are floating on air. Snug but not tight, roughed but soft at the same time. Danny did not take long to decide.

"I will take them."

"You do not want to know how much they are?"

Since his acquisitions days with Albert last year or so, his approach to money has been to spend it wisely and on quality. He knew that this was quality workmanship, but to amuse the kid, he asked how much their shoes were.

"They are $429."

"Great, I will leave them on and head straight to the trail from here."

Jono looked at Danny incredulously. "You are kidding me? You are going dressed like that?"

"What is wrong with the way I am dressed?"

"You are not dressed for a proper and safe hike, mate. You need, even in this nice weather, a good lightweight, breathable and long-sleeved shirt for sun protection. Also, you need pants that are lightweight and quick drying. Add a wide-brimmed hat that will offer you shade and protect your face, neck and ears from the sun."

Danny thought about that and realised the kid was right, but before he could answer him, Jono continued with his litany of requirements to go hiking.

"Of course, you will need sunglasses, which you probably already have, but you also need high SPF for maximum sun protection. Add a good jacket, some merino wicking socks, gloves and insect repellent. That should do it. You got those with ya?"

Danny just shook his head left and right at the kid.

"Alright. Let me go get you all this so you can do a proper hike. Sit here. I will only be a moment."

Ten minutes later, the kid returned with everything Danny would need for *"a proper and safe hike in Australia"* and Jono led Danny to the dressing rooms to get into the clothes. Another ten minutes and Danny comes out looking like Steve Irwin in long pants.

"Now you are ready to go on the trail. We dressed you proper. Come to the front and we will settle."

Waling to the cash register, Danny has his old clothes in a bag, and he hands his AMEX card to Jono and Jono's eyebrow went up a bit, seeing the card. Runs it through the terminal and you see a big smile on him as the word 'approved' shows up on the terminal.

Danny takes his card back, his receipt and walks to his car and a thought popped into his head: *"How did this kid sell me all this stuff? I just needed some shoes."*

A quick look at his watch told Danny he had plenty of time to head back to Crystal Cove, find the trail, walk to the lookout point, take a few photos, and then return in time for dinner at the inn.

As Danny punches the address of the parking lot for the trail, his mind goes in a different direction.

"Was Ms Carter imagining things or did someone indeed go into her room?"

Chapter Sixteen – The Cloud Nine Express Trail

After punching in the directions to the trail, Danny thought about what Jono said about the Cloud Nine Express trail.

Danny was not an avid outdoors person with a passion for adventure. He had never heard about the Cloud Nine Express trail until Gertie showed him the brochure so his anticipation for what was ahead was minimal, however, Jono had sold him a lot of up-to-date gear which he said would more than meet the needs of this trail.

The drive to the trailhead was filled with scenic views, winding roads, and the excitement of what lay ahead. As he approached the parking lot of Cloud Nine Express, he could not help but marvel at the surrounding beauty of dense forests and towering peaks.

Thirty-five minutes later, he pulled up to the parking lot of the Cloud Nine Express to find about a dozen vehicles of all kinds parked, but Danny did not see any of the drivers, so he assumed they were already on the trail.

With his backpack filled with essentials and his new pair of sturdy hiking boots, and the rest of the stuff Jono sold him, Danny sets out.

Upon reaching the beginning of the trail, Danny's excitement quickly turned to confusion. The sign at the entrance declared this to be the trailhead for Cloud Nine Express, but the sight before him did not match the grand expectations he had built up in his mind, nor the photos in the brochure. The trailhead seemed to lead to a path that resembled anything but an "express" route.

This "express" was more likely a slow, agonising crawl through an endless maze of boulders, fallen trees, and treacherous scree slopes. Danny hesitated for a moment, contemplating whether he had made the wrong decision in trying to do this hike, or he misunderstood the descriptions he had read in the brochure. He checked the brochure with its own little map of the Cloud Nine Express, and it confirmed that he was indeed in the right place.

Undeterred by the unexpected appearance of the trail, Danny gave it a shot. After all, he dropped a pretty amount of money on his outfit and hiking shoes, so he entered the trail.

The ascent of Danny began. The rough terrain demanded cautious navigation with every step. It seemed like the trail twisted through thick vegetation, revealing breathtaking vistas now and then, making the effort even more worthwhile.

The name 'Cloud Nine Express Trail' was a playful misnomer. Far from being a swift and easy journey, the trail lived up to Jono's harsh and dangerous description. The name did not even come close to what Danny was seeing as he progress into the trail. This was a rugged, untamed nature of the wilderness. Danny grappled with steep inclines, navigating rocky outcrops, and manoeuvring through dense thickets.

As he progressed, Danny encountered fellow hikers coming in the opposite direction who shared a mix of amusement and exhaustion. The group stopped, introduced themselves to

Danny, and formed an impromptu camaraderie, offering encouragement and sharing stories of their experiences going up on the misnamed trail. Despite the challenges, the beauty of the landscape and the sense of accomplishment was worth it was the common theme from this group, and it fuelled Danny's determination to reach the summit.

Hours passed, and the landscape transformed around him. The slow crawl through obstacles felt like a test of resilience and skill. The trail, though not what he had expected, turned out to be a rewarding adventure, highlighting the raw, unspoiled beauty of nature.

Finally, after a demanding ascent, Danny reached the summit. The panoramic views from Cloud Nine Express Trail were awe-inspiring, stretching as far as the eye could see. A deep sense of satisfaction replaced the initial confusion and scepticisms. Danny realised that the trail's misnomer was a clever play on expectations, inviting adventurers to embrace the challenges and find joy in the journey itself.

As he stood at the summit, surrounded by the beauty of the untamed wilderness, Danny could not help but appreciate the unexpected twists and turns that had led him to this breathtaking destination. The Cloud Nine Express may not have been the express route he had envisioned, but it had become an unforgettable chapter in his trip to Crystal Cove, which will leave him with memories to cherish and stories to share.

The wind whipped Danny's hair into a frenzy as he leaned against the rickety, weathered railing of the lookout point. Below, the world unfurled in a breathtaking tapestry of emerald valleys.

As he leaned against the rickety, weathered railing, Danny's thoughts wandered to building a cabin by the creek. However, a jarring buzz vibrating in his pocket abruptly interrupted his thoughts. Surprised he could get reception this far into the wilderness, he looked at his phone and did not recognise the number, so here answered it: "Hello."

"Danny? Is that you?"

The voice on the other end sent a jolt through him. It was unmistakable, a smooth blend of honey and smoke that had haunted him since he met her.

"Toni? Toni Webster?"

A chuckle crackled through the line. "The one and only. Did not expect to reach you at the top of the Cloud Nine Express Trail the phone reception must be good there. Are you by the old railing looking down?"

A grin spread across Danny's face, tinged with disbelief. Toni was calling him. How did she get his number? He never gave it to her.

"How did you get my number, Toni? I do not recall you giving it to you?"

With another slight chuckle Toni simply said: "I have my sources."

Before he had time to pursue more on the phone number question, Toni quickly asked Danny: "You didn't think to tell me you were embarking on such a...scenic pilgrimage?" Toni teased.

"Danny, the view must be incredible. Tell me about it. Paint me a picture with your words."

For the next hour, the world around Danny faded away. He was not on a rickety lookout point anymore; he was weaving a tapestry of words to recreate the scene for Toni, his voice painting the emerald depths of the valley, the glint of sunlight on the creek below, the whisper of the wind through the trees.

As the sun drifted into the horizon, casting the landscape in a fiery glow, Danny tells Toni he better get back before it gets too dark. Toni sighed. "You know, Danny, you have a way with words. You make a rock sound poetic."

A bittersweet laugh escaped his lips. "And you, Toni, have the power to turn a lonely hike into an unexpected pleasure just by calling me. Well, it is you that inspires me. So, what is your plan for dinner?"

"Nothing I am staying at home tonight."

"How about I take you somewhere for dinner?"

There is a moment of silence and then Toni said: "How about you bring some wine, and I will cook something for you. You like fish?"

"Yes, I do," Danny answers.

"Great, see you at 8 PM then?

"I will be there."

"See you soon Danny, bye," and Toni hangs up the phone and takes a moment to added Toni's number to his address book.

He smiled, the setting sun painting his face gold. He did not know what lay ahead tonight, but the call from Toni had sparked a flicker of hope, a whisper of a melody he had not dared to remember since Alessia.

And as he turned back to the breathtaking view for the last time, the wind carried a whisper of a familiar scent, a reminder that some surprises, like the view from Cloud Nine Express Trail, can turn even the roughest trail into a journey of rediscovery.

Glancing at his watch, he marched down the trail to head back and get ready for his dinner date with Toni.

Chapter Seventeen – An Aroma and a Petal

As Danny headed back to the Poplar Inn to get ready for his dinner with Toni, he noticed the sun dipping below the horizon and casting long shadows across the streets of Crystal Cove. Danny remembered to stop at the local IGA store and grabbed a bottle of Penfolds Bin 28 Shiraz.

As he approached the inn, the warm glow of the inn beckoned him inside. When Danny opened the front door, the familiar scent of polished wood and the murmur of lively conversation from the inn's restaurant greeted him. Danny made his way upstairs to his room, eager to freshen up before the evening.

Upon unlocking the door and stepping inside, he could not shake the feeling that something was amiss. Everything was in its place. His suitcase was neatly tucked away, clothes hanging in the wardrobe, and toiletries arranged on the dresser. Yet, an inexplicable tension hung in the air.

He frowned, his instincts on high alert. Danny took a moment to survey the room, searching for any subtle clues that might explain his unease. The curtains swayed gently, caught in the evening breeze that wafted through the slightly open window. His eyes narrowed as he noticed a faint scent, a subtle perfume that did not belong in the room but one that Danny had experience before. Danny was not sure where, but he was certain he had experienced that aroma before.

He moved further into the room; his senses finely tuned. Nothing seemed out of place, yet an invisible thread of awareness prickled at the back of his neck. The bedspread lay undisturbed, and the room was devoid of any obvious signs of intrusion.

A soft rustle drew his attention in the corner of the room. Danny's eyes focused on a single petal, delicately fallen from a bouquet that adorned the windowsill. He remembered the flowers when he checked into the room. Danny also recalled he never went even close to inspect the bouquet on his first day at the inn.

Examining the petal more closely, he discovered a tiny smudge. He reached for the petal, picked it up and felt the smudge. It felt smooth and fluid, with a lightweight consistency. It was as if someone had gone over to the bouquet and leaned over to smell them, and their face rubbed against the petals and caused the petal to disengage and fall.

A chill ran down his spine as he considered the possibilities. Who could have entered his room? And why? The atmosphere seemed charged with a silent mystery, like a puzzle waiting to be unravelled.

Danny shook off the eerie feeling and focused on preparing for his dinner with Toni. He could not let these subtle disturbances distract him from the evening ahead. Danny placed the petal on his nightstand drawer and decided he would mention what he felt to Gertie in the morning. Yet, as he closed the door behind him, he could not shake the feeling that the shadows in his room held secrets waiting to be revealed.

Chapter Eighteen – Opening Up to Toni

The sun dipped below the horizon, casting long shadows across the quiet suburban streets of Crystal Cove as Danny navigated his way to Toni's house. The gentle hum of the car engine was the only sound breaking the calm evening atmosphere. As he drove, his mind drifted back to the last time he dropped Toni off at her doorstep.

It was just after they had spent all evening at the lake and talked all night long. Danny and Toni had spent the evening together, laughing and sharing stories, their connection growing stronger with every passing moment. When they arrived at Toni's house, she turned to Danny with a warm smile and invited him in for breakfast.

Danny hesitated. The echoes of disappointment from his recent past with Alessia still haunted his mind. They had rushed into things, moving too fast, and it ended in heartbreak. Danny did not want to make the same mistake again. His feelings for Toni were genuine, and he did not want to jeopardise their friendship by jumping into something too soon.

As he drove away from her house that night, Danny could not shake the feeling that he might have let an opportunity slip through his fingers. He cared deeply for Toni, and he feared that his hesitation might have sent the wrong message.

Now, hours later, Danny drove back to Toni's house with a mix of excitement and trepidation. He could not help but wonder if it was time to revisit that moment of hesitation. It was time to take a chance and let Toni in, allowing their relationship to grow beyond the boundaries of friendship.

Parking his car in front of Toni's house, Danny took a deep breath. The memories of that night lingered in his mind, but this time, he was determined not to let fear dictate his actions. As he approached Toni's door, he could not help but hope that tonight would be the beginning of something beautiful, a chapter where he and Toni could explore the depths of their connection without the shadows of past disappointments looming over them.

"Fingers crossed, you better not blow this," Danny thought as he walked to Toni's door.

Danny took a deep breath before ringing Toni's doorbell, his nerves dancing on the edge of anticipation. Moments later, the door swung open, revealing Toni's radiant smile.

"Danny!" she exclaimed, her eyes lighting up. "I'm so glad you're here."

He could not help but returned the smile, feeling a sense of warmth that only Toni could evoke. Before he could say a word, Toni leaned in and planted a big, friendly kiss on his cheek.

"Come on in!" she invited, stepping back to let him enter.

As Danny stepped inside, he could not help but notice the inviting aroma wafting through the air. The cosy ambiance of Toni's home embraced him like an old friend. She led him through the living room and into the kitchen, where he caught a glimpse of the beautifully set dining table.

Toni gestured towards the table with a proud grin.

"How about dinner here, followed by coffee on the patio, and dessert to be determined? How does that sound? The weather is simply perfect tonight."

Grabbing the bottle of Penfolds, Toni pointed to a comfortable outdoor patio with a fantastically large seating area. "Have a seat, Danny. I'll be right back with something special."

Following her lead, Danny walked through the sliding glass doors into Toni's backyard. The soft glow of string lights overhead created a magical atmosphere, and they filled the air with the gentle sounds of the evening.

As he settled into the chair, Danny took in the serene surroundings. Toni returned moments later, carrying the open bottle of wine and two glasses. She poured a generous amount into each glass, her eyes sparkling with excitement.

"To us, having a wonderful dinner and a pleasant evening together," she toasted, clinking her glass against Danny's.

"To us," he echoed, a genuine smile playing on his lips.

Having taken a good sip of the wine, Toni got up and grabbed Danny's hand and said: "Come on, let me show you my backyard."

Toni then guided him through the artfully decorated backyard, stopping at a koi pond that shimmered under the moonlight.

"Isn't it beautiful? I worked hard on this. Well, I helped the landscape designer and pointed to the hired gardener where I wanted everything, even so, it is my garden, born from my imagination," her eyes reflecting the admiration she had for her little oasis.

"It really is Toni and yes, take the credit. It is your imagination that brought it to life," Danny agreed, appreciating the tranquillity of the scene.

After their brief tour, Toni led him back to the patio, where they sat and continued enjoying their wine.

"Danny, may I ask you a question and please, if you do not want to answer it, please, just tell me and I will not press you."

That statement surprised Danny, but he had been thinking about where this new relationship might be going. True to his nature, he wanted to be upfront and honest about himself.

"Please go ahead Toni, ask away."

"The other day when you dropped me home after we had such a lovely time on the Crystal Cove Lake and I asked you in for breakfast, why did you hesitate?"

Danny took a deep breath, the weight of his past decisions settling on his shoulders. He met Toni's gaze, his eyes revealing a mix of vulnerability and regret.

"Toni, that early morning when you asked me in for breakfast... it wasn't about you. It was about me and my own fears," he admitted.

"You see, before we met, I was in a relationship with someone named Alessia. Things were going well, or so I thought, until I made a big move. I asked her to marry me."

Toni's eyes widened in surprise, and she reached for Danny's hand, offering silent support.

"But she didn't say yes," Danny continued, his voice tinged with sadness. "That was over nine months ago. Instead, she left without a word, and I have not heard from her since. She just disappeared, leaving me with a lot of questions and a heartache I didn't know how to cope with."

Toni squeezed his hand gently, offering comfort. "I did not know, Danny. I'm sorry you had to go through that."

He managed a small smile, appreciating Toni's empathy. "It was a tough time. My best friend Albert said I needed to get over her, to take time off from work, and so here I am in Crystal Cove. I was not sure if I was ready to open myself up to someone again. When you invited me inside that morning, all those fears and uncertainties came rushing back, and I hesitated. I didn't want to make the same mistake again, and I didn't want to hurt you."

Toni nodded, her gaze soft and with a smile that showed she understood.

"Thank you for sharing that with me, Danny. I can imagine it was difficult. And I appreciate your honesty."

As they sat in the night's quiet, Toni felt a deeper connection forming between them. Danny's vulnerability had opened a door to understanding, and Toni knew they were navigating the complexities of their pasts together.

"I'm here for you, Danny," she whispered.

Danny smiled, grateful for Toni's understanding. The weight he had been carrying seemed lighter, and the promise of a fresh start hung in the air.

"And I'm glad we can talk about these things. It is a new beginning for both of us, and we can take it one step at a time and go as fast or as slow as you want. Sharing my deepest feelings with you has helped me understand how I feel. Toni, I hope you understand.

"Danny, I understand. Thank you for opening to me. Now I promised you a nice dinner. How about we go inside, and you help me finish cooking it?"

With that statement, Toni again took Danny by the hand and led him inside.

As they walked into the house, Danny felt a weight lifted off his shoulders and he knew he was now ready to continue their conversation, allowing the night to unfold and their connection to grow stronger with each shared moment.

Chapter Nineteen – A Better Time

An aroma infuses the kitchen with the delectable fragrance of herbs and spices as Toni and Danny prepare dinner. They cluttered the countertops with fresh vegetables and herbs as the beautiful swordfish laid on the cutting board.

Whisking a marinade Toni asked: "Danny, tell me what you did today?"

Danny smiled as he chops the carrots for tonight's dinner.

"After our late night, I slept in and had a French toast breakfast that Samuel made for me, for lunch…."

"Samuel made you French toast for lunch?"

"Yes, he did, and it was delicious. Afterwards I asked Gertie what she would recommended for me to, and she gave me a brochure for the Cloud Nine Express trail and suggested I get the right equipment for the trail up in Byron Bay which is where I headed and dropped a few dollars on hiking boots and other assortments that the young man at the store convinced me I need. He was right. I needed all that stuff."

"Then, as I am enjoying the view from the lookout point, I hear a wonderful voice on my mobile number inviting me to dinner. Little did I know I would have to work for it."

"Do not be a baby," a smiled Toni said. "There is something therapeutic about preparing a meal together.

"Absolutely. Especially when you have fine wine with the labour. So, what is the secret ingredient for our swordfish marinade tonight?"

"Well, I thought we could go with a citrusy marinade with lemon, lime and a hint of orange zest. It will give the fish a refreshing kick."

"Sounds perfect. I noticed your small herb garden. Do you need anything from there?"

"Good Idea. I was thinking about fresh rosemary. It will add a nice earthy flavour. I am also thinking of roasted veggies with a balsamic glaze. What do you think?"

"You are the chef Toni, but I love that idea. The sweetness of the balsamic would complement the savoury flavours of the fish."

They continued to work together seamlessly, Toni marinating the red swordfish while Danny continued to chop vegetables for the side dish. The sound of sizzling and chopping fills the air.

"You know, I read that cooking together strengthens relationships," said Danny with a little smirk.

"Is that so? Well, I am all for strengthening our relationship, especially if it involves delicious food, a better understanding of each other, and spending more time together."

"Do not work get a bottle or two of vino," added Danny.

Toni and Danny share a laugh as they continue working side by side, the warmth of the kitchen and the joy of shared effort creating a cosy atmosphere and savouring the wine as they work.

"You know Danny, I also read that read that couples who cook together stay together."

With a big smile, Danny responded, "Well, in that case, we're in it for the long haul."

This time they both laugh loud, and Toni lets off a snort which makes them both laugh even more.

As they put the finishing touches on the meal, they fill the kitchen with the delightful aroma of the swordfish and roasted vegetables. Toni and Danny share a satisfied look, proud of their culinary creation.

They take all the dishes to the table and start eating and enjoying the last drops of the wine.

"Danny, do you want some more wine?"

"Yes, please. What do you have that will go well with the swordfish?"

Toni gets up and goes to her small wine shelving and comes back with a 2021 Reserve Pinot Noir from the Yarra Valley.

"Please let me open it," said Danny as he reaches for the bottle.

Danny is impressed.

"Toni, did you buy this vintage, or was it recommended for you?"

"This one was recommended. Why?"

Opening the bottle and smelling the cork, Danny cannot help himself and said: "You realise it has an excellent garnet red colouring with a complex and beautifully balanced layers of fresh and dried fruit and spices. Excellent choice to whoever recommended it."

"You know your wine as well, Danny. Are you a connoisseur of wine?"

"No, I love drinking it."

As dinner progressed, the soft glow of candlelight bathed the dinner table as they sat across from each other, enjoying the symphony of flavours and textures spread before them. The ambiance is serene, and the air is filled with the gentle occasional clinking of cutlery.

"This wine is exquisite," said Danny, taking a sip of wine. "Now Toni, you tell me, are you a wine connoisseur or do you rely on recommendations?"

"OK, you got me Danny. I dabble. It's amazing how a superb wine can enhance the entire dining experience. What about you? Any hidden talents I should know about?"

Danny thought if he should share his acquisition talents with Toni. He wanted to be honest, but he thought it would be better to wait for a better time.

"I'm afraid my talents are more in the realm of bibliophiles appreciating more than creating. Although, I make a mean bowl of corn flakes."

"A mean bowl of corn flakes? I have a box around the house somewhere," said Toni with a small chuckle. "Maybe you can share your secret recipe for it."

"Perhaps. But only if you promise not to reveal my culinary secrets," said Danny with a big grin.

The conversation pauses momentarily as they savour the last few bites of the meal. A delicate dance of flavours unfolded on their plates, and for a moment, words take a back seat to the final sensory experience.

"Tony, that was one magnificent meal. Is there nothing you cannot create?

"I was told that there is a visitor in Crystal Cove this week that has a tremendous recipe for serving Corn Flakes."

They both laugh at that statement.

"You know, Toni, I've always believed that beauty is in the details. Just like in life, it is not just about the big moments; it's about the nuances that make each day special. Starting out the day with a bowl of corn flakes makes for a beautiful experience."

"Danny, you have a poetic way of looking at things. It's refreshing."

"I find life more interesting that way. What about you, Toni? What's your philosophy about the trivial things?"

Toni taps her fork thoughtfully and said: "Life is a mosaic of moments. Each one contributes to the overall picture, and it's our job to appreciate the artistry in the chaos."

"Darn, that is deep, girl."

Again, they share laughter.

They continue their leisurely conversation and exploring topics ranging from travel to literature. The evening unfolds with an effortless rhythm, the subtle exchange of glances and the nuances in their words creating a connection that goes beyond the surface.

Grabbing her glass and wine bottle, Toni tells Danny to leave the plates, come outside to the patio and enjoy the evening breeze and to continue their conversation.

Danny laughs and grabs his glass and follows Toni to the patio. As they get settled in, Danny asks a question which has been on his mind for a while.

"Toni, I've been meaning to ask you something. Have you been in a meaningful relationship before?"

With a smile and running her finger on the wine glass, she said: "Well, you know, relationships are a bit like recipes. Some turn out great, and others… not so much."

Trying to keep the question light, Danny continues the question, but is in a lighter mood.

"I like that analogy. So, spill the beans. What's your relationship history like?"

Taking a thoughtful sip, she answered him: "Honestly, before you, I let no one get too close. I was always the perpetual singleton, convinced that I was better off alone."

Raising an eyebrow, Danny cannot believe that but cannot help to said: "Really? Hard to believe someone as amazing as you?"

"Appearances can deceive, Danny. I was always busy with work, convinced that my independence was my strength. But then you happened."

"Ah, the infamous me." pointing to himself, he added: "What was it about this guy that changed your perspective? You realise it only has been a few days since we met."

Looking into Danny's eyes Toni answered his question: "Yes I realise that Danny but you, my dear, are a game-changer. Your kindness, your patience, the way you understand me without words... it made me realise that, just maybe, being vulnerable isn't a weakness. That night on the lake we spoke a lot, and shared a lot, and tonight we continued sharing. This is something I never done, not this deep, with another man."

"Well, I'm honoured to be the one who has reached you, but tell me why you kept everyone at arm's length before?"

"I guess fear overwhelmed me. Scared of getting hurt, of losing my sense of self in someone else. I've seen too many relationships go south; you know? But with you, it felt different from the start."

Leaning closer to Toni and gently Danny said: "Different in a good way, I hope?"

Nodding, Toni simply said: "Different in the best way possible. You made me realise that finding someone special can happen in the most unusual circumstances and that I do not have to compromise on love. It can be an addition, an enhancement."

They share a moment, the weight of Toni's revelation lingering in the air. The subtle sounds of the evening surround them, as if their newfound understanding of each other's pasts will make their relationship easier to share.

"Toni, I am going to be here for a couple more weeks. I am hoping for you, and I to share more times together, if it is OK with you?"

"Yes, I would like that very much."

"Would it be too much to ask if you could take some time off work so we could spend more time together?"

Toni reflects a moment on his questions, takes a sip and gives Danny the answer he hoped for: "Yes, I believe I could ask for a week off, even on short notice."

"Will that present a problem? I do not want you to feel obligated I realise I am asking a lot and so soon into this relationship. We are having a relationship, right?"

"Danny, I'm confident there won't be any problems. Our connection is in its early stages, but it's already quite profound. I want to take our relationship to the next level by requesting a week off at the inn tomorrow. I trust that Gertie and Samuel can handle things, for I have been training Milo as a backup chef, and I believe he's well-prepared for the task."

"Oh. I do not think I met him yet."

"No, you probably have not. He does not come out of the kitchen often."

"How is he working out for you?"

"Like me, he started out at the bottom and learned quickly, but then again you got to start somewhere, and he has done an amazing job of learning all I have taught him during his apprenticeship. I believe he is ready and what better reason there could be? You are asking me to take a few days off, I have accrued many since working at the inn and it is time for Marcus to step out of the shadows, sort off, and get ready to take over if I ever choose to leave."

"And are you leaving?"

"No. Not yet. I have no reason to leave just yet."

Danny looks at his watch and remarks: "Look, I best be heading back to the inn. Let me help you with the dishes and cleanup and then I will head out."

"Goodness, you are right, it is 2 AM. Where has time gone?" said Toni, looking at her watch.

"Let me walk you to the door. I will clean up. I can sleep in," and Toni gets up and takes Danny's hand to walk him out.

As Toni opens the front door and Danny turns, she gives him a long and passionate kiss and after she said: "Thank you for sharing your fears with me and letting me into your life, Danny."

Danny smiled and only responds with a simple: "No, thank you for listening," and he turns and heads towards his car as Toni gently closes her door.

Chapter Twenty – New Hope

As Danny drove back to the inn under the blanket of the starry night, he could not shake the warm glow that enveloped him. The winding roads echoed the twists and turns of the conversations he had shared with Toni just moments before.

His fingers tapped rhythmically on the steering wheel, replaying the moments when they had exposed their souls, exchanging stories of past heartaches and triumphs. Each shared revelation lifted the weight of unspoken emotions, deepening their connection.

The soft hum of the engine provided a comforting backdrop to the realisation that Toni's laughter had become a melody that repeated in his mind. The road ahead stretched out, mirroring the possibilities that seemed to unfold between them. Her voice carried a quiet confidence as she expressed a desire for more time together, leaving Danny with a sweet anticipation.

As the headlights cut through the darkness, Danny could not help but feel a sense of renewal.

The road back to the inn represented more than just a physical journey; it mirrored the path they might navigate together in the future. The promises of shared adventures and the prospect of building something meaningful were deep in his thoughts.

His mind raced with different thoughts about the evening's conversation.

"Am I moving too fast?

"Am I expecting too much, too soon, from Toni?

"Does she feel the same way I do? Of course, she does. She is going to take time off from work. That counts for something, right?"

"Did I make the right choice by not sharing my past relationship with Albert and our acquisitions over the years? What would have been her reaction to this truth?"

A gentle smile played on his lips as he approached the familiar façade of the inn, knowing that the threshold he was about to cross held the potential for something beautiful.

As he turned off the ignition, Danny took a moment to absorb the quiet satisfaction that welled up within him. Tonight, had been more than just another late night. It had been a bridge, connecting the past to the present and paving the way for a shared future.

With a heart full of hope and a mind buzzing with the echoes of their shared laughter, Danny stepped out of the car, ready to embrace the new chapter that awaited with new hopes.

Chapter Twenty - One - Surprise

Danny was able to get just six hours of sleep, for at 10 AM sharp, his mobile rings and the familiar mobile handle 'Hair Man' shines through the phone screen.

"Good morning, Albert. How are you?"

"Sweetness, you sound like you are still in bed. Are you alone?"

"Yes, I am. What's up?"

"Nothing. Things are going so smoothly here that I thought I give you a ring and see how you are doing. Why are you in bed still? You are not feeling well?"

"As a matter of fact, I am feeling wonderfully, Albert. I had a dinner date last night, and it went spectacularly."

"A dinner date, you say. Tell me all about. Do not leave out any minor detail tell me, tell me."

So, for the next fifteen minutes, Danny related his dinner date with Toni, the happenings of the night at the lake the previous day and last night.

"You said you did not mention our past activities, which I agree with you. It is something that you should say nothing about."

"I am not sure Albert. I really like this lady and I do not want to start off on the wrong foot with her. If she later finds out about it and confronts me, what do I say to her then? Any ideas?"

"Oh, Danny sweetheart, I do not understand women, so I am not a useful source of knowledge on the subject. There is a possibility that if you tell her, it will not go as smoothly as expected.

"I get your point, Albert. I think I should tell her, but at the right time. Albert, please give me a second there is another call coming through," prompting Danny to put Albert on hold, and he sees it is Toni.

"Hi Toni."

"Good morning, Danny. Glad you are up. Listen, I just spoke with Gertie and Samuel. They are ready to let me have a week off, seven days, and allow Marcus to solo at the inn. So, with that in place, how about we drive somewhere today? How does that sound to you?"

"It sounds simply great, Toni. How about you think of a place to have lunch and I will pick you up at 1 PM for lunch? How does that sound like?"

"Sounds perfect. See you at one and I know exactly where to go for lunch. It is exotic and expensive I hope you do not mind?"

"Not at all. See you soon."

Hanging up, Danny returns to Albert.

"Well, you kept me on hold for a while. Who was it? Was it your new lady interest?"

"Yes, it was. We are going out to lunch, and we will spend more time together since she just asked for and received seven days off from work."

"Oh darling, good for you. You need a brief distraction and from what you shared; she sounds divine. I cannot wait to meet her. I will come down over the weekend."

"No, you will not. I need to develop a closer relationship and you are too nosey, Albert. Besides, I am sure you do not want to do the long drive."

"You are right. I hate long drives alone. So, take care and speak to you soon. Have fun and if you have too much fun, do not name it after me," and Albert lets out a loud laugh and hangs up on Danny.

Looking at his watch, Danny knows he has plenty of time to get ready to pick Toni at 1 PM, but he also wants to speak with Gertie about his feeling that someone has been in his room.

After shaving and showering, Danny goes for a classic look. He goes for a pair of dark wash jeans with a maroon button-down shirt and dress shoes. Then, Danny takes the petal he found with the smudge, puts it in his pocket, and, satisfied with his appearance as he looks at himself in the mirror, he goes downstairs.

Finding Gertie behind the reception counter, he starts his conversation with a friendly salutation: "Hello Gertie, how are you this day?"

"Well, if it isn't Mr Danny Monk, the thief."

Startled by that statement, Danny does not know how to react but then Gertie adds: "Oh, do not act so surprised. You are taking Toni away from us for a week or so. You could have waited for a better time, but then again, she had worked hard, and she deserves some time off. I am expecting you to treat her nice. Many people here in Crystal Cove love her.

"Of course, Gertie. I will treat her in the manner she should be accorded. Sorry your statement took aback me."

Gertie laughed a bit and said: "Just a joke Danny. Not too many men get time with Toni. You must be special."

"Well, thank you for that. Now Gertie, may I ask you something?"

"Of course. How may I assist you?"

"The other day there was a guest speaking with you, concerned that someone had been in her room. Do you remember?"

"Of course, I do. I told the guest no one goes into the rooms that are not allowed to do so. Why do you ask?"

Taking the petal out of his pocket, Danny shows it to Gertie.

Gertie looks at the petal as if it is a strange object, looks at Danny, back to the petal and simply asked: "It is a petal. What about it?"

"You notice the smudge on it, Gertie?"

Taking a second good look this time, and picking up the petal, Gertie examines the petal closer and indeed sees the smudge and replied to Danny: "Yes, I do now. What is it?"

"It looks to me like a foundation or makeup. Somehow it got on the petal as if someone has smelled the flower, skimmed the petal with his or her face and nudged the petal of its stem."

Gertie is still confused.

"Danny, what are you trying to tell me?"

"It is my opinion that someone has also been in my room, looking around, saw the vase with the flowers, took an interest, smelled the flower and unnoticed to him or her, clipped the petal from its stem and left some of his or her makeup or foundation on the petal."

"When did you find this petal?"

"Just the other day."

"Hold one moment," and Gertie goes and gets a mobile phone from behind the reception desk, dials a number and Danny hears: "Robert, can you find Alice, Becky, and Bian and the four of you come to the reception area, please."

"Let check my staff and see if any of them wear this type of foundation or makeup right now. I am intrigued by this."

"Gertie, I did not wish to get your staff in trouble I was just wondering if you knew who might have been in my room the other day."

"Well, one of these four employees would have been in your room, but we do not log in who does which room each day. They get done by whomever is ready to do it, so I will have to ask."

In a few minutes, the staff arrived and stood next to me, waiting for Gertie to ask them a question.

"Who cleaned Mr Monk's room yesterday?"

I looked at all the staff.

Robert was out, for he wore no foundation nor makeup that I could tell and while the ladies did indeed wear some makeup, it was not of the same tone as the smudge on the petal, so I did not think the culprit stood in front of me.

"I cleaned Mr Monk's room, Mrs Bailey," said Becky.

"By any chance, did you clean around the flowers in the room? Did you smell the flowers?" asked Gertie.

Looking a bit confounded by Gertie's question, Becky simply shook her head and said: "No, I cleaned around the floor of the windowsill where the flower was, but I did not smell the flowers for any reason. Why?"

"Just curious Becky. Mr Monk, do you have a question for Becky?"

"Yes, I do. Becky, did you notice anyone hanging around the hall before you went into my room? Maybe a guest or someone else you do not recognise?"

"No sir. There was no one in the hall when I went into your room. Did I do something to upset you, sir?"

"No, Becky, you did nothing wrong. Like Gertie said, I am simply curious. Thanks Gertie, I have no more questions for your staff. Sorry for the bother."

"Not at all, Mr Monk." Gertie gestures for the staff to continued working and said, "Back to what you were doing." As they leave the reception area, she turns to Danny and asked, "Who do you think might have been in your room?"

"No idea Gertie, but it is a coincidence that just the other day, what was her name," and Gertie interjects: "Mrs Carter," "Yes, Mrs Carter was speaking to you about the same matter. I do not believe in coincidences."

"Should I be worrying about that? Is one of my staff lying to me? They all have been with me for years."

"No, I do not believe they are responsible. Robert wore no makeup and the three ladies had makeup or a foundation on, but I could tell it was not a match. Has any new guests checked in since I checked in?"

"None. Everyone was here when you arrived. Why?"

"Just wondering Gertie. Let us keep this between us, OK?"

"Can I share our conversation with Samuel? He needs to know what is going on in his establishment as well."

"Of course, please do share with him, but let us make sure not too many people are aware of what is happening. The fewer people who know, the better, for we may catch who is going into your guest's rooms."

Danny looks at his watch and quickly added: "I need to be going. I am having lunch with Toni, and I need to pick her up. I will see you later, Gertie.

"Have a pleasant lunch. Know where you are going?"

"No, Toni said she has a surprise for me."

"Wonderful, I, for one, love surprises," added Gertie.

As Danny turns to head off to his car, he wonders about what surprise Toni has for him.

His mind just thinks of two questions: *"Who is meddling in the guests' rooms and why?"*

Chapter Twenty-Two – Echoes of Love

Danny had no issue in finding Toni's home and arrived a few minutes before 1 PM. As Danny approached the door, anticipation, and curiosity filled his mind. The atmosphere was charged with a mix of nervous excitement and the unknown. As he raised his hand to knock, the door swung open unexpectedly, revealing Toni standing there. A warm, genuine smile illuminated her face, instantly putting Danny at ease.

In a surprising and affectionate gesture, Toni took the initiative. Stepping forward, she gently placed her right hand on the back of Danny's head, drawing him into a tender embrace. The touch was both reassuring and intimate, creating a connection between them. As she leaned in, Toni pressed her lips against his, and time seemed to stand still.

The kiss was filled with a sense of familiarity and sweetness, leaving Danny with a feeling of warmth that radiated through his entire being. It was a moment of genuine connection and shared emotion, making him feel not only desired but also appreciated. Danny couldn't help but appreciate the beauty of the unexpected encounter and the delightful sensation that enveloped him during that heartfelt kiss.

After the lingering kiss, Danny finally took a step back, a content, and genuine smile spreading across his face. The atmosphere between them was charged with a newfound closeness, and the air seemed to sparkle with shared joy. Breaking the silence, Danny couldn't help but comment on the delightful surprise.

"Well, a good afternoon to you too," he said, his voice laced with a hint of playfulness. A light chuckle accompanied his words, expressing both amusement and a sense of appreciation for the unexpected but welcome gesture.

Toni, catching onto the playful tone, responded with a mischievous glint in her eyes. "I thought it was time to add a little excitement to your afternoon before lunch," she replied, her voice carrying a playful cadence. Her response reflected a shared sense of humour and a comfort in their connection.

The exchange created an easy going just right for Danny simply said: "You ready for lunch? What's the name of this expensive place you're taking me?

"Oh, it is not far. Let me get my purse and lock up. Wait for me in your car I will be out in a second."

Danny walked back to his car and stood next to the passenger door for Toni. The kiss, the atmosphere, broke any potential tension that might have lingered after last night. Danny thought it set the tone for a continuing positive and enjoyable interaction, hinted at the promise of more delightful moments to come.

After a few minutes Toni comes out and Danny gets a good look at her. She looked, how would Albert describe it, smashing, yes smashing would be the word.

His attention was drawn to the dress. The midi length elegantly framed her figure, accentuating her curves in all the right ways. The explosion of vibrant colours and eye-catching floral print couldn't go unnoticed, engulfing him in a wave of summer bliss. He might imagine her twirling in it, the fabric swirling like a kaleidoscope against the backdrop of a breezy day.

Toni opted for a pair of stylish and comfortable sandals in a neutral colour which elongated her legs and made her look almost regal.

The sandals added a touch of summer flair with a woven straw tote bag. It looked like she was carrying all of her essentials in it, and yet it added a relaxed touch to the outfit.

Toni knew how to complement her dress with just a dainty necklace and one bracelet. Her gold watch complemented the warm tones of the dress.

"*Smashing, simply smashing*," thought Danny as he opened the car door for Toni, who seemed to slide into the front seat with ease.

Toni closes the door and goes around to the driver's side, gets in, and asked: "Where to for lunch Toni?"

"A mystery place, just twenty-five minutes away. Let me punch the address into your GPS, may I?"

"Of course," and Toni punches the address, and the GPS starts its command on how to get to the mystery location.

"You will not tell me what this expensive place is?"

"It is a surprise, Danny. I am sure you will enjoy the cuisine. Come on drive. I'm hungry. What kind of music do you have in this thing, anyway?" Toni said as she meddles with the radio system.

Following the instructions from the GPS, Danny drives and sees that the GPS is indeed stating that the location is twenty-two minutes away, and wonders what Toni has in store for him.

Toni finds a playlist labelled "AV" and plays it.

Danny listens to the songs, songs that Alessia had selected to be their songs. Should he stop the playlist or let them play?

Before he could decide, Toni said: "What an interesting choice of songs, Danny. You have Andrea Bocelli: '*Con te Partido*', then you have Al Green with '*How do you mend a broken heart*,' followed by Gregory Porter with '*It's probably me,*' quite an assortment of songs and there is an even more interesting collection. What made you choose them?"

"I did not choose them, Toni. Alessia did."

Danny thought that his statement was going to put a damper on the ride and the conversation, but Toni simply said: "I like her choices. There is a quirkiness I can relate to with the mix of songs."

Hearing Toni say that relaxed him for the rest of the ride. Toni Webster has accepted Danny Monk's past echoes of love without hesitation and moved forward. Danny was confident that they would have a pleasant lunch wherever they were headed.

Chapter Twenty - Three - Magia

GPS announces they had arrived.

The neon sign of "El Gordo Meat Pies" buzzed and flickered like a disco ball in hangover aftershocks. Danny blinked, adjusting to the mystery lunch that Toni promised. Danny was expecting a chic little bistro instead, he got this, well, ahem establishment.

Walking inside, the air hung thick with the intoxicating aroma of caramelised onions, savoury gravy and a hint of fryer oil that would not be out of place at a monster truck rally. A mismatched symphony of polka music and Spanish pop blasted from a boombox propped on a stack of empty pie boxes.

Behind the counter, a rotund man with a handlebar moustache that could double as a gravy mop smiled like a mischievous Buddha. "Welcome, amigos! You look famished. What can I tempt you with?"

"Uh, well," Danny stammered, his vision still trying to adjust from Toni's dress to the collection of plastic gnome figurines adorning the counter. "We were hoping for something... refined?"

Toni chuckled; her eyes sparkling. "Relax, Danny. Trust me, this is where the magic happens."

El Gordo's grin widened. "Toni, you call it magic. I call it *Sally's 'magia.'* Good to see you again. Who is this muchacho?"

"Tomas, this is Danny. I am treating him to the best you have to offer."

Danny cannot help but said: "You know each other?"

"We go back to culinary school in France. I failed. Toni became a success and fate brought us together in this beautiful part of the world when I met my life partner, Sally Allen. Sally is the chef of 'El Gordo Meat Pies' and I am the brains," Tomas said, laughed.

"What does Sally have cooking up today, Tomas?" asked Toni.

Pointing to a table, Tomas ushers them and with a chuckle makes his suggestion: "I recommend you go with Sally's 'Chupacabra Chorizo'! Spicy chorizo, caramelised onions, and a secret ingredient that will make your taste buds tango. I also would add two 'Estrella' cervezas from Barcelona to give it that 'classy, refined atmosphere' Danny was looking for."

"That sounds fantastic. Bring us two of each," answers Toni and winking at Danny she added: "You will not regret it."

Tomas finds two beers and brings them to the table, and he then winks as he returned behind the counter and launched into a dramatic flourish with a pastry brush, slathering a golden glaze onto a behemoth of a pie.

Bring them the two pies and placing them in front Tomas simply said: 'Salud' and leaves them alone.

Danny raised an eyebrow, but one bite in and his scepticism vanished faster than a politician's promise. The crust - flaky, buttery, and shatteringly crisp. The filling - a molten river of spiced chorizo and caramelised onions, each bite an explosion of savoury, sweet and a hint of fiery kick. It was a pie that sang opera on your tongue, a culinary tango that left you breathless and begging for more.

Before finishing their first pie, Toni raised her hand and motioned to Tomas for two more and then two more.

As Danny devoured his third "Chupacabra Chorizo", his initial reservations had morphed into pure, unadulterated bliss. He glanced at Toni, her mouth dusted with pastry flakes, eyes glowing with mischievous delight. In that moment, amidst the polka music and gnome figurines, he realised she was not just showing him a hidden gem, she was showing him another side of her, an adventurous, fun-loving side that thrived on unexpected detours and greasy spoons with the best darn pies in Australia.

So, while *El Gordo Meat Pies* might not have had white tablecloths or sommeliers, it had something far more valuable: magic, or 'magia', as Tomas said, in its pies, laughter in the air, and a memory that would forever be etched in Danny's taste buds (and probably his arteries), a testament to the day his expensive lunch date took a delicious nosedive into the heart of greasy spoon nirvana.

Chapter Twenty - Four - Diet

"I would have never thought I would have had such a delicious lunch in this hole in the wall place," remarked Danny as they walked out the 'El Gordo Meat Pies' out of earshot of Tomas towards his car.

"Shush Danny, you do not want Tomas to hear you and for sure you do not want Sally to hear you as well. Good thing she was in the kitchen busy."

"Well, I have to say that the calibre of the meal indeed surprised me. Are all the small establishments and eateries this good around the area?"

"There are few and you been lucky to eat at another 'hole in the wall' eatery that Gertie recommended, remember?"

"Wait a moment. Your place, the Seashell Café, is not a hole in the wall. I would not say that."

"Let me correct you, Danny. The Seashell Café is my mother's place, not mine. I just happened to be there the day you waltzed into my life while I was helping."

"I waltzed in?"

"Yes, you waltzed in. I saw you the looking around the café, soaking up the atmosphere just to make sure you would be comfortable inside."

"So, you spied on me?"

"No, I had stepped outside to the counter to speak to my mother and was walking back to the kitchen when you came in and you caught my eye."

"I see, I caught your eye," and Danny does a quick twirl as he gets to the car and does a little bow.

"Did I pass inspection then? How about now?"

"You are being silly. I did not mean you caught my eye like 'you caught my eye.' I just saw you out of the corner of my eye when you walked in."

"Well, Toni, you have nice eyes."

She reprimands Danny with a quick slap on his arm, said, "Stop it."

Danny opens the door and Toni gets in and before Danny can close the door she asked: "Danny, are you up for a coffee and dessert?"

"Sure. What have you got in mind?"

"Get in and I will tell you."

Danny closes the door and wonders if Toni is going to take him to another hole in the wall establishments or surprise him with something completely different.

As he closes his door and starts the car Toni is busy inputting a new address in the GPS and suddenly a voice emits: "Turn right onto Broward Street."

"Another surprise?

"Yes, Danny, another surprise. Drive my chariot driver, drive."

"Yes, milady," as Danny heads to the road and turns right.

The GPS said it was a forty-minute drive to the address. Danny did not ask. He had plenty of petrol and he did not mind driving, for it meant he had more time to speak with Toni or just listen to music. Toni had found Bay FM on the radio at 89.9 and it played the latest modern music. Danny was not really a fan, but Toni likes it, so Danny nodded his head to the sound of the beat as he drove. He would have preferred some of his old favourites, but like the old said goes: 'when in Rome'.

"Danny, tell me about your friend Albert. What is he like?"

"Why do you want to know about him?"

"Well, you spoke a little about your parents, then a bit more about the gentleman you purchase your bookstore from, Mr McCullum, but you have mentioned albert a lot in our conversations but not really said much about him."

"So, what do you want to know?"

"As much as you can in the next twenty minutes or so we have until we arrive."

Danny was not sure how to really explain Albert to Toni. Albert is albert, and it is best to meet him in person and draw your own conclusions, but he thought he would give Toni an airplane view of the man.

"To start, Albert ran what was an institution in the whole of Sydney. He had established a reputation for offering the best hairstyles through the arduous work of his eighteen-person crew, all individually trained by Albert. This eye for perfection made *'Cut Me Crazy,'* that was the name of his hair salon, the envy of all hair salons in Sydney. His ten chairs are always full of prominent citizens from Sydney, the local area, local, and national politicos, and celebrities, all of them wanting to be pampered by Albert's staff."

"How exciting. Did you ever get your hair by Albert?"

"No, I went to Josh's Place for my haircut."

"Why?" asked Toni, amazed at Danny's answer.

"Josh charged me thirty dollars and at albert's place, his folks charged one-hundred-sixty dollars."

"One hundred and sixty dollars for a man's haircut? What did they do for that type of money?"

"Well, the male hairdressers, they were not called barbers, would welcome you with their waistcoat-wearing outfit, then they would place a warm, dry towel on the customer's neck to get the customer comfortable. Then they would start with a hair wash and to relax you even more a five-minute head massage before you sat on the chair for your haircut. At this point, you would get a choice of a brandy, a cognac or a Scotch to sip whilst getting your haircut. A simple haircut, mind you, but Albert had taught them to be like a surgeon with their scissors. When they finished with you, not a single follicle would be out of place. The place was always packed with men wanting their hair done."

"But not you?"

"No, not me?"

"Again, why not?"

"Loyalty Toni, loyalty. I had been going to Josh ever since he open his two-man chair shop on Main Street next to Mr McCullum's store when I was going to high school. He always did right by me, and I will continue to go to him until he retires."

"When will he retire?

"Well, he is seventy-four now, so I figure, maybe another ten years or so."

"Or before he chops off an ear, right?"

"Yeah, that also could be a potential reason," Danny chuckled at Toni's response.

"At the round-about, take the second exit and you will arrive at your destination on your right in one kilometre," the voice from the GPS stated.

"Ah, almost there, quick, tell me more about Albert," remarks Toni.

"OK, Albert is 173 cm tall, slender, with a weight of just sixty-nine kilos, give or take a few, with perfectly coiffed blond hair, and the most beautifully manicured hands to rival Cleopatra. His blue eyes resemble the ocean and what truly marks him as unique is, of course, his outfits."

"His outfits?"

"Yes, let's say if there is ever an invention that could control the brightness in a man's outfit, Albert would be the perfect individual to be the spokesperson for the product."

"That wild?"

"Yes, but in his defence, he wears it well like the song says."

"What else can you share about Albert Danny?"

"Albert was the first to welcome me to Mr McCullum's employment and even tried to recruit me as an apprentice. While his recruitment failed, our friendship blossomed over the years and when I bought the business even more with words of encouragement and financial advice."

"He tried to recruit you to work as a hairdresser?"

"Yes, he did, but it was not for me."

"So, you ended up a little old bookshop owner."

"Who are you calling old?" and Danny does an air slap on her knee, which draws a giggle from Toni.

"You arrived at your destination."

Danny pulls into the shopping centre's parking lot and reads the welcoming sign: *'Salvatores Gelato and Coffee.'*

Danny's only thought is: *"Boy, I am glad I am not on a diet."*

Chapter Twenty-Five - Suspicious

Salvatores Gelato and Coffee looked like an Italian gelateria that pays homage to old-world practices, but with a very Australian style to it. With a mix of rustic hand-rendered walls and some decorative vases overflowing with seasonal flowers to evoke a coastal atmosphere there is a stuff koala and kangaroo mounted on the wall. It made for an interesting view of the tiny establishment.

Stepping inside, Toni and Danny grabbed a table, and the server came up instantly with a menu.

"I will grab you a bottle of water and two glasses. Please look at the menu and let me know what I may serve you," and she walked away to get the water.

"My, she is chirpy," said Danny.

"Would you not be chirpy, as you put it Danny, working in such a lovely place," Toni answers while looking at the menu.

It was Danny's turn to look at the menu and he saw Salvatores had quite a selection.

"Wow, they just about cover the colours of the rainbow when it comes to flavours and the number of options for coffee is mind-boggling. How can a person choose? What do you recommend, Toni?"

"It depends on what you are interested in. I have had about everything in this shop. From their apple, cinnamon, and almond; or strawberry, hibiscus tea, and mint sorbets, which are served in a fancy, refined dark doe brown, colour adorned bowl with the retro Sixties pattern that cost a fortune, do not break them for they cost about $130 each, or you can go with the more mundane options of a choice of a cone, or a cup."

Danny shows Toni his hands and said: "With these clumsy things, I think I am going with a cone and a traditional flavour mango."

"An apple sorbet for me and I am going with their Panamanian espresso."

"A Panamanian espresso? Never heard of it. What is it like?"

"I was told once that the coffee beans are from a single origin bean variety grown only at the base of the El Valle volcano in Panama, which gives the beans a unique flavour. You should try it. That is, if you like espresso."

"I do and I will once the young lady returns," and if by orders from the coffee gods, the young server appears.

"Hi again, here is your water. My name is Liza, with a z. Are you ready for your order?"

Danny gives the order for the sorbets and lets Liza, with a z, know they will have a coffee as well, but will order the coffees when they finish eating their sorbets. Liza is happy with that and walks away to place the order.

"So, after sorbet time and coffee time, what else is there to do in this part of the world, Ms Webster?"

"I was thinking about that and since the sun sets late, I thought we see an interesting, but touristy place. Are you game?"

"What place do you have in mind, Toni? Is it close by?

"It is, but we will have to get changed, for we do not have the attire for this trip."

"What are you thinking of doing that we require a clothes change, Toni?"

"Have you heard of the Nightcap glow worm cave?"

"No."

"The cave is in a lush rainforest which we need to have the clothing for the walk to get to the cave. Are you game?"

Danny did not have to think too long if it meant more time with Toni he would fly to the moon, so he said: "I am good to go."

"Here are the gelatos. Enjoy. I will return when you finish for your coffee order," said Liza.

Looking at Toni for approval, Danny asks Liza to give them five minutes to enjoy the gelatos and place the order for two Panamanian espressos. Liza nods her approval and goes away.

The gelatos, as Toni suggested, were just delicious. Salvatore Vincenzo, the namesake of the establishment, brought the traditional gelato-making technique with him when he emigrated to Australia sixty years ago. They have handed the secret down from generations of Italian gelato makers in the Vincenzo family.

After savouring the gelatos and as if my providence, Liza shows up with the two espressos, which again were of lovely and distinctive taste.

After paying for their order Danny and Toni decided Danny would drop off Toni at her place giving her an opportunity to change, and then he would head back to the inn, change as well, and return to pick her up and head over to the Nightcap glow worm cave.

Arriving at the inn, Danny heads to his room and sees Abe standing by Danny's door.

"Abe. What's up?"

Abe jumped, startled by the sound of his name being called out, turned, and looked at Danny.

"Oh, hi Danny. I..., I was about to knock to see if you were in and would like to grab a coffee downstairs."

Danny looked at Abe closely.

In the middle of the afternoon, Abe was wearing slim black anti-slip sweat-proof sensitive and breathable fibre gloves. Danny knew of these gloves, for he has worn them a few times in the pass during some of his, and Albert, acquisition ventures. *"What was up with Abe,"* Danny thought to himself.

Trying not to be obvious to Abe that he noticed the gloves, Danny just gives him a quick answer: "Sorry Abe. Meeting up with Toni to go see a cave. Maybe in the next day or so we can grab a coffee. OK with you?"

"Sure, sure Danny. Please, you and the chef enjoy yourselves. We will catch up soon," and Abe removes his gloves as if it is the most natural thing to do and puts them in his coat pocket and heads towards the stairs.

Danny watches Abe as he goes down the stairs and makes himself a mental note to do a bit of research on Abe Reynolds when he has a moment without Toni. Opening the door to his room, Danny just has the feeling that Abe was attempting to go into or out of Danny's room and not about to knock on the door.

Danny seldom relies on gut feeling, but this time he could not stop himself from thinking that there was indeed something suspicious with Abe's actions.

Chapter Twenty-Six – A Good Place

Danny arrives at Toni's place and before he has a chance to turn off the car to walk to her front door, the door opens and out comes Toni.

The outfit Toni is wearing tells Danny she has done some hiking prior to today. Toni is wearing what Danny can describe: a forest green open-air pants with multiple pockets which are practical, functional, and comfortable at the same time. Her top is a sea olive colour long sleeve hoodie which colour coordinates wonderfully with the pants. She is holding in her hand a straw hat, which is SPF 50+ rated specifically for the Australian sun. Even in a rain forest, it is advisable to have SPF protection. Danny recognises the style and the brand of her hiking boots: a Salomon hiking boot just like his own. Oh, yes, she did this before.

Not waiting for Danny, Toni gets in the car, takes control of the GPS, and puts in the address.

"I called ahead and made a booking for us, so no need to hurry. We are taking a guided but abbreviated tour of the rainforest and the waterfall, and then the cave. "

"Is there much hiking to do?" asked Danny.

"Some. We will park your car and then the tour guide will take us on a trail until his vehicle no longer can traverse and then we walk for about two kilometres through the rainforest until we reach the waterfall. At that point, we take a few photos," see said batting her eyelashes at Danny in jest, "and then we take the walk into the cave, which is about one-half kilometre from the waterfall. The cave itself is not too large but deep, damp, and cold, so I am glad you dressed appropriately."

"How long will this take, Toni?"

"The abbreviated tour is only two hours because we do the trip through the rainforest by cutting through some shortcuts. It normally is a six-hour tour, an entire day event, since it includes lunch."

"How much is it?"

"All taken care of, sweetie. My treat after that exquisite and exotic lunch at 'El Gordo' and the dessert at Salvatore's."

"Great, I like a woman of means," said Danny, grinning.

It did not take long for them to arrive at the departure point for the tour. After checking in, they were introduced to their guide: Fabricio, a young exchange student that has been doing this for a few years during his summer breaks from university studies. He spoke perfect English and after a few housekeeping points for safety and making sure we had water etc, we headed to the vehicle to start the tour.

Fabricio knew the route because he drove like a madman through the worn trail and Toni and Danny were glad, they had worn their seat belts for they were bouncing like Mexican beans until Fabricio stop the vehicle and told them the next part of the tour would now start and it would be on foot.

As they start their walk Fabricio starts his dissertation which he probably has memorised over the years: "The park is on the south-eastern edge of the Mount Warning erosion caldera, you know what a caldera is," looking at us and we both nod to the affirmative, and he continued. "All of gullies, ridges, and peaks form the eroded remnants of the Tweed shield volcano. The tallest peak at Nightcap is Mount Burrell, also known as Blue Knob, with an elevation of 933m above sea level. OK, so far, not confusing?" he asked, stopping, and looking straight at them.

Again, both Toni and Danny respond with a node and a strong 'yes.'

"The basalt and rhyolite lava that once flowed from the Tweed volcano erupted over 23 million years ago, and produced various vegetation communities you see around us. The park receives rainfall exceeding 2500mm per year, but it seems you picked the perfect afternoon as there is not a cloud to be seen in the sky."

As Toni and Danny followed Fabricio, he continued explaining more facts about the park such as the forty species of mammals, twenty-seven types of reptiles, twenty three different frog varieties, and over one hundred bird species that make the park their home. Fabricio also shared that the park contains over six hundred plant species, but all Danny could do was be enthralled with the beauty of the rainforest as they walked towards the waterfall, which Danny could hear even at this distance.

"Careful now, now comes a bit of tricky and rocky trail to get to the waterfall but once you get there, you will see that it was worth the effort," Fabricio states.

Fabricio was not exaggerating the roughness of the rocky trail but he did not mention that it was a short one for shortly after starting, Danny and Toni reached the lookout platform for the waterfall. Fabricio makes a triumphant announcement: "Lady and gentleman, I give you Minyon Falls."

Danny almost gasped. The view from the Minyon Falls lookout was spectacular. Danny could see the not only the falls themselves and the valley beneath. The day, being clear and not a cloud in the sky, allows for a glimpse of the far away coast.

Toni comes up to Danny's side and together they enjoy the sounds of local wildlife, the peaceful ambience, and the spectacular natural surroundings. She takes his hand, gives it a squeeze, and gets on his tippy toes, and places a kiss on Danny's cheek.

"What was that for?" Danny asked.

"You look like a little boy seeing his favourite toy for the first time."

"It is an amazing view, Toni. You were here before?"

"Yes, many years ago. My mother and I took the same tour, but we had an older gentleman doing it for us and it was a bit more boring. Fabricio seems to be really into the nature part of the tour, and I really enjoyed his explanations as we hiked up here."

"He did a good job indeed." Was all Danny could say as he continued lookout out to the forest below full of Australian eucalypts, blackbutt, and scribbly gum, and at the beautiful pool at the base of the waterfall, which looked like an ideal place to cool off and relax.

"That pool looks so inviting. Too bad we did not bring out swimmers," Danny said.

"Who needs them?" Toni responds with a mischievous smile.

"OK lady and gentleman, time for me to bring you to the cave. This way please. Watch your steps as we leave the lookout point area."

Ten minutes later, they arrive.

It was not a cave, but a man-made tunnel.

"Fabricio, this is not a cave," Danny protests.

"Correct. It is an old railway line, but we call it a cave, since it seems more poetic once you get inside."

Thinking it was a bit of false advertising, Danny said nothing back and just followed Fabricio, then Toni, into the tunnel.

They must have walked a good eight-hundred metres and Danny's eyes were just getting adjusted to the darkness when he saw most glow worms. And there were loads of them!

The glow worms seemed to favour damp spots and there were some big clusters of twinkling blue lights in the alcoves along the sides of the tunnel and, of course, across the ceiling.

Danny followed the lead from Fabricio and kept stopping to look up and making sure he had turned off his torch. Danny felt he was standing under a brilliant night sky. The worms were not along the whole of the tunnel's ceiling, but in enormous masses. As he stood in the middle of the tunnel, Danny reached over and grabbed Toni's hand and they both looked up. The best effect from the worms was in the middle of the tunnel, Danny thought.

They stood there in the dark looking up and could not resist giving each other an enthusiastic kiss.

"We will have none of that people. The glow worms will get ideas," and they both busted out laughed at Fabricio's comment.

After a few more minutes Fabricio said: "OK, it is time we head back. Let walk slowly back the way we entered and be sure you go slowly so your eyes adjust to the outside light."

As they began their walk out of the tunnel, Danny felt he was in a good place.

Chapter Twenty-Seven – Wild Rumours

Danny and Toni walk back to the car after Fabricio has dropped them off at the tour office.

"What do you want to do for dinner, Danny?"

"No plans Toni. Do you have any suggestions?"

"I have yes. Are you game for another surprise?"

"If it is as good as the last few, yes, count me in."

"OK, take me home so I can freshen up and come back to get me at 8 PM, OK?"

Danny nodded and, as the sun dipped below the horizon, casting long shadows across the winding country road. Danny and Toni continued their animated exchange. Their other conversations had touched on everything from childhood dreams to the intricacies of string theory, or at least what they both learnt from watching episodes of 'The Big Bang Theory,' seemed to crackle with an electric spark, each new topic igniting fresh bursts of laughter and thoughtful ponderings.

Reaching a stoplight, Danny glanced at Toni, her profile bathed in the soft glow of sunset. A smile played on her lips, her eyes sparkling with an unreserved enthusiasm that warmed him from the inside out. He felt a sudden urge to pull over, step out into the twilight, and simply savour this moment of pure connection.

But the light turned green, pulling him back from the precipice of spontaneity. He resumed driving, a melody of possibilities humming in his mind. Should he invite her later for an impromptu picnic under the starlit sky? Or suggest their first movie date, the shared popcorn a metaphor for their blossoming bond? *"Were there any movie theatres in Crystal Cove?"* he thought.

Instead, the words that tumbled out surprised even him. "So," he began, a slight tremor in his voice, "would you like to help me solve the mystery of the missing sock drawer key?"

Toni's brow furrowed in mock confusion. "What key?"

He chuckled, his nerves calming under her amused gaze. "You know, the one that unlocks the portal to an infinite realm of lost socks. Legend has it, only the chosen one can wield it..."

"I do not understand Danny. What key? What sock drawer?"

"One of my favourite authors, J. F. Nodar, wrote a short story about a missing sock drawer magical key that enables anyone who holds it to find all their missing socks thus reuniting all those odd, unmatched socks you keep in your sock drawer."

And just like that, they were off on another adventure, dreaming of a fantastical tale that would have banished the last remnants of the day's anxieties, if they had any to begin with. The drive home, initially a simple route in familiar surroundings, morphed into a whimsical journey through a world conjured from shared laughter and unbridled imagination.

When they finally reached the familiar façade of Toni's house, the early evening held a different meaning. It was not just the end of another day, but the beginning of something new, exciting, and laced with the sweet promise of untold stories yet to be told: their first 'dinner date' and a surprise dinner date, at that.

Arriving at Toni's Danny gets ready to turn off the car when Toni touches his hand and said: "It's OK Danny, I can get there by myself," and gives Danny a quick peck on the cheek as she opens the passenger side door and heads towards her door, stopping to see if there was any post and runs the last few steps to the front door. Inserting the door key, Toni opens the door, turns around and waves at Danny.

Danny waves back and puts the car in gear and heads to the Poplar Inn to freshen up himself and get ready for dinner.

Waling in, Danny glanced around the dimly lit interior of the Poplar Inn and notices Samuel walking towards him.

"Danny, will it be possible to have a moment together?"

"Sure Samuel. How can I help?"

Samuel points to Danny to go over the side of the restaurant, away from the former patrons. Danny wondered what could be so urgent that Samuel needed to speak with him in private. The inn's patrons chattered and clinked glasses in the background as Samuel led Danny to a secluded corner.

"What's going on, Samuel?" Danny asked, his curiosity piqued.

Samuel glanced around cautiously before lowering his voice. "There's trouble brewing, Danny. Several guests, including yourself, have stated that there seems to have been someone in their room. They all say nothing has been taken but that they can tell someone has been in the room."

"I see Samuel. Have you noticed anything yourself?"

"Nothing. Ghosts have set their sights on the Poplar Inn."

Danny furrowed his brow, concern etching his features. "Ghosts. Really? What do they want here?" Danny said with a smile.

Samuel sighed, his eyes darting nervously. "I am not saying they are ghost Danny it just seems because people are sensing, something but not one person has seen anything strange."

"OK Samuel, I have a strange question for you."

"Sure. What is it?"

"Has anyone been asking questions about an old legend like a hidden treasure rumoured to be buried on the grounds of the inn? Or may that many years ago a pair of lovers died here, and their souls are trapped, hence the ghosts?"

Samuel's eyes widened. How did Danny know? The legend of the hidden treasure had been a local myth for generations, passed down from one resident to another. No one had ever found it, but the mere mention of it stirred excitement and curiosity.

"There is an old rumour about hidden treasure on the grounds, Danny. How did you know? Did someone share the rumours with you? Or did you read it somewhere?"

Danny smiled, for he was just as surprised as Samuel. He had heard nothing, but greed is always a great motivator, and a hidden treasure makes greed fun. "No, Samuel, none told me anything, I just guess."

"Why would they come looking for it now?" Danny wondered aloud.

Samuel shook his head. "I don't know, Danny, but people hear a whisper about hidden, buried treasure and they become, well, crazy."

As Samuel spoke, Danny's mind raced. He had grown up in a small town and knew every nook and cranny of it and while hidden, buried treasure was never a legend in Northport, the old stables had ghosts, or at least, that was the rumour so why not Crystal Cove have buried treasure.

"We can't let the guests start wild rumours," Samuel declared. "We need to gather the guests, come up with a reasonable reason for their feelings, and make sure we lay everything to rest."

Danny nodded in agreement.

"I knew I could count on you, Danny. I will ask the guests at breakfast. It is the one time all are in one place at once, tomorrow for their opinions and get any updates. Can I count on you for breakfast? Let us rally the folks and figure out how to deal with this situation before it escalates any further."

"Of course, Samuel," looking at his watch Danny explained to Samuel he needs to get going for he had a dinner date.

"I see. Toni has kept you busy these past few days. We rarely see you at dinnertime here."

Danny smiled and pointed to the stairs, and Samuel just smiled and nodded.

Rushing upstairs, Danny could not shake the feeling that this conversation that Samuel had proposed with all the guests would test the guests' patience.

Unlocking his room door, Danny looked around and sensed nothing this time, so maybe it was just a feeling the last time, but then he spotted the petal on the floor with the makeup or foundation smudge on it.

Danny quickly showered, shaved, and, looking at his watch, noticed he had time for a quick beer downstairs.

As he exited his room, he saw Abe Reynolds coming out of his room.

"Abe," Danny called out.

Abe turned around and waited for Danny to reach him.

"May I buy you drink Abe downstairs? I have a few minutes before I head off to a dinner date with Toni, the chef. My treat."

"Young man, you said the magic word: treat. Let us enjoy a drink downstairs."

Little did Danny know that the events about to unfold would not only challenge him, Toni, the owners of the Poplar Inn, but also uncover long-buried secrets and lead to unexpected results.

Chapter Twenty-Eight - Reactions

Danny and Abe walk downstairs and head into the bar section of the restaurant and sit at the bar when, as if by magic, Samuel appears.

"Gentlemen, what may I serve you?"

Danny, still startled by the sudden materialisation, blinked twice. "Uh, hey there," he stammered. "Samuel, you would not be, like, a genie, would you? Because we did not actually rub any lamps..."

Abe, ever the pragmatist, chuckled. "Easy there, Danny. Maybe he was under the bar checking on something?"

Samuel, a hint of amusement twinkling in his eyes, chuckled to himself. "Indeed, gentlemen. Your friendly neighbourhood bartender and inn owner, at your service. Though I assure you, my appearance harmed no lamps." He gestured around at the shelves stocked with colourful bottles. "What tickles your fancy? A classic bourbon, perhaps? Or something more...adventurous?"

Danny, recovering his composure, straightened his shirt. "Maybe something to steady the nerves," he admitted, glancing at Abe's raised eyebrow. "Double tequila sunrise, if you can swing it."

Abe, shaking his head but smiled, leaned on the counter. "Whiskey neat for me, thanks. And make it a good one, Samuel.

You have some marvellous stuff here? You seem awfully...smooth behind the bar."

Samuel winked. "One learns a few things after a few...episodes. Let us just say I enjoy a delightful story, and yours, gentlemen, promises to be quite the narrative. Now, who is ready to spill?"

As Abe took a swig of his whiskey, and Danny nervously stirred his tequila sunrise, the air crackled with anticipation. Where was Samuel heading with this conversation? Did he find out something about the entries into the rooms? Did he have some suspicions? The conversation, it seemed, was just getting started.

"I never spill a drink, Samuel," joked Abe, holding his drink steadily in his old hand. "How about you Danny? Do you spill your drinks?"

"Only when I dance," Danny answered.

The air hung heavy with unspoken questions. Danny's playful answer only highlighted the underlying curiosity about Samuel's enigmatic remark. He shifted on his stool, the tequila sunrise refracting a kaleidoscope of colours in his eyes.

"So, Samuel," Danny broke the silence, his voice tinged with apprehension, "what did you mean by...spilling? Are you, uh, looking for a confession? Some juicy gossip?"

A smile danced on Samuel's lips, his gaze flitting between the two men. "Gentlemen," he drawled, a playful glint in his eyes, "information, like good alcohol, is best savoured, not shaken. I would not dream of forcing a story. But...let us just say I appreciate a well-told yarn, one woven with a touch of mystery, perhaps a dash of danger."

He leaned in, lowering his voice conspiratorially. "Heard any whispers of a shadowy figure lurking about town? Perhaps a clandestine meeting gone wrong? A stolen artefact with ancient secrets?"

His words hung in the air, a spark igniting curiosity in Danny's eyes. Abe, however, remained stoic, taking a thoughtful sip of his whiskey. "Now, Samuel," he interjected, "we appreciate the theatrics, but you are talking to seasoned adults here. We deal in facts, not fairy tales."

Samuel chuckled, a warm, rumbling sound that echoed in the dim bar/restaurant. "Facts, my friend, are often the most fantastical stories of all. But believe what you will. Tell me, gentlemen, do you find yourselves drawn to these whispers? Does the intrigue tickle your adventurous spirit?"

Danny, eyes alight with a sudden spark, looked at Abe. A silent communication passed between them, a flicker of excitement battling against caution. Perhaps Samuel was just an eccentric bartender inn owner, but the possibility of adventure, however shrouded in mystery, was undeniably tempting.

"You know what, Samuel?" Danny grinned, the tension in his shoulders easing, "tell you what. Why don't you spin us a yarn? About yourself, about this town, about these whispers you speak of. And maybe, just maybe, if your story's good enough, we might have one of our own to exchange."

A slow smile spread across Samuel's face, crinkling the corners of his eyes. "Ah, now that is the spirit! A trade of tales, eh? I like the sound of that. But be warned, gentlemen, my story might leave you thirsty for more than just your drinks."

He swirled a cloth around a glass, the clinking catching their attention. The bar, it seemed, had just become a stage, and Samuel, the enigmatic bartender inn owner, was ready to play his part. Where would his story lead them? Would Danny and Abe reveal their own secrets in return? The night, filled with the scent of bourbon and whispers of mystery, was just beginning when Gertie walks in.

"Samuel, are you bothering Mr Reynolds and Danny?"

"Gertie, you take out all the fun of working behind the bar," said Samuel sheepishly.

"Gentlemen, is he enticing you with some type of intrigue? Asking you trade tales? My husband is a troublemaker, that he is, so whatever he has asked you to share, it was all in jest. Just to make conversation."

"Well, he did a marvellous job for I for one was ready to bite," said Abe.

"And what would you have shared with Samuel and me, Abe?" Danny asked.

"I am not saying anything now since Samuel is now out of the picture in storytelling," Abe said with a smile.

"So, no secrets Abe?"

"Secrets, probably a few that need to remain secret. And you Danny?"

Danny thought on how to answered Abe. He had secrets. Everyone does. Some can be shared while others it is best for them to stay secret. Besides, Gertie said Samuel was just making a jest. Poking fun.

"No, not one secret. An open book. After all, I own a bookstore."

"In that case, thanks for the drink, Danny. I am heading out. Speak to you later," and Abe nods to both Gertie and Samuel and leaves the bar/restaurant.

Danny waits until Abe was out of earshot and asked Samuel: "Samuel, were you just joking around, or did you have some intention with this mysterious approach to get us to speak?"

Samuel nudges Gertie closer to him and leans to Danny.

"Bian came to me this morning and said she thought she saw Mr Reynolds coming out of the Wentworth's room."

"Is she sure?"

"I asked her that and she said she was not one hundred per cent sure, but it looked as if he was closing the door quietly behind him. When he saw her, he did not say a word. Just smiled at her and continue to his room as if nothing had happened."

"Now I understand you asking us to spill. You hoped he might slip and say something incriminating."

"Yes, that was my intention, but I did not share with Gerti, so when she came into the bar and asked if I was bothering you two, I played along. Not make a massive thing out of it."

"Are you still planning on having the group conversation in the morning?"

"Yes, I am. I think I need to."

Looking at his watch Danny said: "Samuel, Gertie, I need to leave for my dinner date with Toni. I will let you take the lead in the morning, and I will backup you if I can in the morning. How is that?"

"Good Danny, I appreciate it. This mysterious incident needs to stop. I plan to leave a small note in each room saying breakfast will be at 8AM tomorrow instead of the normal time that way everyone will be there at once. I will also have all our staff there at the same time. Have fun and see you in the morning."

"Good idea Samuel. Please put the drinks on my tab. See you soon."

With that, Danny left to pick up Toni and wondered how the morning breakfast was going to go with Samuel, raising the concerns of some of the guest. *"It will be interesting to see Abe's reactions,"* thought Danny as he walked to his car.

Chapter Twenty-Nine – There is Always Tomorrow

Danny arrived at Toni's home and found her outside, waiting for him. As he stopped the car, she motioned to him not to get out and rushed over to the passenger door, opened it, and jump inside.

Danny's heart stuttered, momentarily thrown off by the playful glint in Toni's eyes. In the fading light, he could almost detect a hint of mischievousness under the early moonlight illuminating her face. He feigned mock disappointment, a smile tugging at his lips. "Toni, you scared me half to death! I thought you were being chased by angry blue tongue lizards."

Toni feigned a gasp, clutching her chest dramatically. "Blue tongue lizards? My dear Danny, you wound me! This is a sophisticated surprise, not a rodent rendezvous." She pointed towards a picnic basket she tossed on the back seat, its wicker body radiating a warm glow from the fairy lights hidden inside. "Now, let me buckle up, because I'm directing you on an adventure."

Intrigued and relieved by the light-hearted turn of events, Danny obeyed. As they sped off, he noticed they were not heading towards any restaurants he recognised. Curiosity simmered, but the playful anticipation in the air was infectious.

Following Toni's instructions, the car weaved through winding back roads, eventually stopping at a secluded clearing bathed in moonlight. Getting out, Toni quickly spread a blanket on the soft grass awaited them, alongside a small wine cooler. She turned on a Bluetooth speaker playing soft music radiating from her phone, and she quickly took out the fairy lights and strung them between the trees, creating a magical canopy.

"Ta-da!" Toni announced, beaming proudly. "Your personalised, blue tongue lizard-free dinner date, served under the stars."

Danny was speechless. The thoughtfulness and effort, not to mention the sheer whimsy of it all, warmed him from the inside out. "This is incredible, Toni. Thank you."

Taking his hand, she led him towards the blanket. As they settled down, she revealed the picnic basket's contents: gourmet cheeses, fresh fruits, crusty bread and the chilled bottle of wine. Laughter filled the air as they shared stories, savoured the delicious food, and danced under the starlit sky.

Later, curled up under the blanket, gazing at the Milky Way, Danny admitted, "You may have scared me at first, but this... this is the best surprise I've ever had."

Toni squeezed his hand. "The best is yet to come," she whispered, pulling out a small velvet box. "Remember that time you said you wished on a shooting star for a lifetime of adventures with me?"

"At the lake the other night," Danny said.

Danny's breath hitched. He knew what was coming, and yet, his heart hammered with anticipation. As Toni opened the box, revealing a delicate silver ring engraved with a tiny shooting star.

"Would you like to embark on that adventure with me, Danny?" she asked, her voice soft.

Putting on the ring, all Danny said was: "More than anything, Toni. More than anything."

admired the ring on his hand, he asked: "How did you get my ring size?"

"I guessed. I am good with jewellery."

"Indeed, you are Toni."

"Danny, I got a strange call from Samuel just before you arrived. He asked to be at the inn for an 8AM breakfast meeting. Do you why? He said to ask you."

As Danny related what Samuel had explained to him and Danny shared his own concerns, you could see Toni's face change from glee to concern.

"You think it is one of the staff? I would never do that."

"No Toni, I do not think is one of the staff that would be way too obvious, but then again, I might be wrong. One thing I know it is not you. That is for sure."

A smile radiated from Toni's face.

"Thank you for that."

Some of the fairy lights started flicking, showing the end of their battery life.

"Danny, would you mind taking me home a bit earlier than I want to? I need to be sure I am there for the 8AM meeting. I will see you in the morning, yes?"

"Of course, Toni," as they both started pick up the remains of the surprised night picnic.

Under the watchful gaze of a million stars, their surprise dinner date ended sooner than planned. Whatever promised the night sky might have in mind did not transpire, but Danny thought: *"There is always tomorrow."*

Chapter Thirty – Mi Media Naranja

They arrived back at Toni's house. Once again, Toni asked Danny not to inconvenience himself by escorting her to the front door. She gave Danny a long, sweet kiss and when Toni opened her front door, she turned and blew him a kiss.

Acting like a young teenager, he 'clutched' the kiss in the imaginary air and placed his hand on his heart.

Arriving at the inn, Danny quickly went to his room, intending to give Toni a quick goodnight call, when, upon opening the door, he noticed a note under the door.

Quickly reading the note, Danny smiled and can only think he is going to be involved in an Agatha Christie mystery with one of her protagonists at the morning's breakfast when his phone rings and he notices the name: 'Hair Man.'

"Albert. What a delightful surprise. Is everything OK?"

"It is, darling. I just wanted to call and let you know I will also take a few days off and I was wondering if you would like some company up there with you in Crystal Cove?"

The question hung heavy in the air, laced with concern and a hint of doubt. Danny heard when Albert shifted his weight, a slight creak of his floorboards.

"Oh, darling, I get why you are worried. But trust me, I would not be asking to see you if it was not important."

Danny walked over to the window, peering out at the looming silhouette of Crystal Cove against the darkening sky.

"You say you are OK but will not say what your concerns are over the phone, and you want to see me. Albert, it sounds like you are in trouble. Are you?"

"Nonsense, darling. Everything is fine at 'Albert-Albert Hair Salon'. I just need to discuss something with you. The business side of the business and it is always better over a nice dinner and a glass of wine. Besides, I might get to see your new love interest as well. Right?"

"Of course," thought Danny. Curious Albert cannot wait to meddle, but then again, gaining a friend like him is not easily done.

"OK Albert. I will make a booking for you in the morning. I think they might have a room available for you."

"Not to worry sweetness, I already made the booking. My accommodation room is at the Driftwood Den. The person who handled my reservation informed me that they had decorated the room with weathered wood and natural textures, giving it a rustic, beachcomber ambiance. The room has my private entrance. I will access a small garden that offers a serene outdoor environment, perfect for unwinding and immersing myself in the invigorating sea breeze. How delightful."

"You booked it already! You were confident I would say yes to you coming up. Were you not?"

"Aye cariño. You know you are like 'mi media naranja, my other half.' I know you better than you know yourself. See you in the morning. Ciao!" and Albert hangs up.

Looking at his watch Danny decides not to call her and let her rest and speak with Toni in the morning.

With that decision out of the way and Albert's hanging up Danny is left to ponder what Albert would need to talk about that cannot be done over the phone or wait until Danny's return to Northport.

"Let's see what mess Albert has got into when I was not there," Danny said aloud as he got ready for bed.

Chapter Thirty-One – A Sneaky One

Danny had a wonderful night's sleep. Waking up refreshed and eager to go to Samuel's breakfast meeting with the rest of the guests.

"Maybe I should have taken some time beforehand to discuss with Samuel the best approach at this Hercule Poirot style meeting," Danny said aloud while he shaved.

After a refreshing shower, Danny looked at his watch and saw the time: 7:49AM.

"Perfect," he muttered to himself as he walks out of his room, heading towards the stairs. Suddenly, there is a conga line approaching the stairs.

Danny sees the Wentworth, Mr and Mrs Maxwell, and Ms Lititz Carter leisurely ambling towards the stairs. He called out.

"Good morning, ladies and gentlemen. Ready for breakfast?"

The group simultaneously turns and look back at Danny and Sally smiles and simply said: "Good morning, Mr Monk. My, you are a morning person, are you not?"

"Indeed, I am Mrs Wentworth. A good night sleeps does that to you."

"So, the mysterious note from Samuel for this breakfast meeting did not perturb you?" asked Mr Maxwell.

"Not one bit. Maybe Samuel has a surprise for us. A game of sorts. Who knows? Shall we all go downstairs I for one am getting hungry?"

With that, everyone went down the stairs and found Abe Reynolds outside the closed restaurant door.

"Good morning, everyone. It seems we cannot go in. The door is locked."

"This is going too far," exclaimed Ms Carter. "I need my breakfast I have things to do today. Places to go to. People to see."

As if by providence, the door opens wide with Samuel welcoming all.

"Thank you for your prompt arrival. Breakfast is now served."

The guests all walked over to their customary tables. *"Humans are such creatures of habit,"* thought Danny as he too headed to his usual table and sat with Abe Reynolds.

"You know what is going on, Danny? What is all the theatrics about?"

"No idea Abe. Let us hear what Samuel has to say."

Danny looked around and quickly saw that Samuel had gathered all his staff over in one corner. Looking weary, there stood Robert, Marie, Allison, Marcus and the housekeeping staff: Alice, Becky and Bian and to Danny's surprise, a middle-aged man in a suit. *"That suit reminds me of Detective Cassell,"* Danny thought to himself.

A moment later, out of the kitchen door comes out Gertie with Marcus and Toni on toe. Toni sends a quick wink at Danny, which catches him by surprise, and he just smiles at her.

"It seems we are all here now," Samuel exclaimed.

A hush fell over the room as Samuel cleared his throat. Danny observed the faces of the assembled guests, their expressions ranging from nervous fidgeting to indignant defiance.

"Dear guests," Samuel began, his voice as crisp as a starched collar, "we find ourselves in a most curious predicament. Last night, Mr Reynolds reported that his Tag Heuer Carrera watch vanished from his locked room."

Murmurs erupted amongst the guest and staff alike. Mrs Maxwell and Ms Lilitz both clutched their respective necks, making sure their necklaces were still there.

Danny observed Abe was expressionless and, indeed, was not wearing a watch. Danny searches his memory and does not recollect Abe wearing a watch when they first met, but was it a Tag Heuer Carrera?

"How can this happen, Samuel? How can this happen, Gertie?" asked Jim Wentworth, "Doesn't the front door have security measures after 11PM, allowing only guests and staff with access keys?"

A heavy thunderous voice behind Samuel said: "Some things defy even the strongest lock, sir. Perhaps Mr Reynolds just misplaced his watch."

"Ladies and gentlemen, allow me to introduce Detective Liam Callum. He was informed last night of this gathering and has come to interview each of you with a few questions while you have breakfast. He has already interviewed me, Gertie, and the rest of the staff. Enjoy your breakfast and I am sure this will not take too long."

"Bingo. Detectives must get a discount for their suits somewhere in NSW," thought Danny as he observed as discreetly as he could the scene being played in front of him. His keen eyes missed no detail as he surveyed the room filled with intrigue and suspicion. A sense of unease settled over the guests as they realised that one among them stood accused of pilfering the precious timepiece.

Detective Callum, unfazed by the murmurs and guest theatrics, raised a hand. "Ah, I will prepare and someday my chance will come," the detective said, stopping all conversation and many of the breakfast activities.

Sitting down with Jim and Sally Wentworth, the detective spoke aloud: "This little quote, is attributed to Abraham Lincoln, and covers, in my opinion, the many opportunities anyone can have to act in a manner that another individual may not detect."

The room did not go completely silent with the detective in the room, but it was not as boisterous as normal. Danny looked at Toni, who no longer was in the room and must have gone into the kitchen. The rest of the staff had also dispersed to go about their normal activities, leaving on Samuel in the corner watching all.

After a few minutes, detective Callum left the Wentworth's and sat with Ms Lititz Carter, and she looked quite uncomfortable the moment the detective sat down.

"What do you think the detective is asking the guests? Would his questions be any different to the questions he must have asked the staff already? What do you think, Danny?"

"Not sure, Abe. I have had brief interactions with the authorities."

"Well, the Wentworth's seemed to have been quite successful with their answers for the detective did not stay long with them and Ms Carter, she certainly looked uncomfortable to me when the detective sat down, well she looked that way to me, anyway. Any thoughts Danny?"

"My opinion was that the Wentworth's were truthful with their answers and knowing that Gertie and Samuel must have given the detective some background, being honeymooners and all, the detected probably asked the questions he needed at this time."

"And Ms Carter?" interjects Abe.

"Ms Lititz Carter is always comfortable."

Abe giggled at Danny's remark and then nodded to him.

"Look, the detective has finished questioning Ms Lititz Carter and is now heading towards Mr Aloysius and Mrs Evelyn Maxwell. Let us watch their reaction."

Danny did not bother to look at Mr Aloysius and Mrs Evelyn Maxwell reaction but at Abe's reaction to the detective's enquiries as the detective went from table to table.

As the detective sat down with the Maxwells, Danny watched him as well. The detective seemed intelligent, alert, eyes that proved as he asked questions. smiled to himself Danny thought: *"A young Hercule Poirot but without the moustache and the Belgian accent."*

"You got a smile on your face, Danny. Thought of something you can share?"

"No Abe just thinking to myself, and it made me smile."

"Look at Homer Witham. He looks guilty to me just sitting there. Does it look like he is twitching, you think, Danny?"

Danny looked at Mr Witham and yes, he looked uncomfortable more than everyone else, but then again, he is awaiting trial for fraud, so I guess anyone would be if a police officer sat down to interrogate you.

"Abe, based on what you told me about his impending court case, his demeanour could reflect that anxiety. It does not make him guilty."

"Well, if we get to vote. He has mine," responded Abe, taking a sip of his coffee, and suddenly putting his cup down.

"Look Danny. It seems it is our turn now," as detective Cullum, heads toward Danny and Abe.

The detective appears friendly and smiles as he sits down and introduces himself. "Good morning, gentlemen. My name is Detective Liam Callum. I need to ask you a few questions. First, may I have your names?"

Both Abe and Danny introduced themselves.

"Excellent. Mr Monk, would you mind going to the bar with your coffee since you have finished your breakfast while I speak with Mr Reynolds? When I conclude my questions with him, I will ask him to go to the bar and then you can return to your seat. Is that, OK?"

"Of course, no problem, Detective Cullum."

As Danny sat down on the bar, Toni comes out of the kitchen.

"Danny, I have been watching the detective go around the room. Any idea who might be the thief?"

"My, oh, my Toni. How did you see all that?"

"Well, I did not see, but as each plate was being served by Allison, she would come back and let met us know what was happening in the kitchen."

"And you are not worried about Samuel seeing you here now with me?"

"Not one bit. I have kept both Gertie and Samuel aware of our activities these past days."

"All our activities Toni?" Danny asked with a slight smirk on his face.

"Not all of them, you naughty man. What a mind you have?"

Danny was getting comfortable speaking with Toni when she interrupted him. "Danny, I think it is your turn now. The detective is waving at us."

Looking quickly, Danny sees that indeed the detective was waving at him as Abe was heading toward the bar and as Danny and Abe crossed, Abe just said: "Be careful Danny. He is a sneaky one."

"A sneaky one," thought Danny, as he sat down for his own interrogation.

Chapter Thirty-Two – Albert and His Timing

Detective Callum leaned back in his chair, steepling his fingers in front of him. His gaze was steady, assessing. "Mr Monk," he began, his voice a smooth baritone, "would you like to tell me why you were at the scene of the crime last night?"

Danny swallowed, suddenly aware of the scratchy fabric of the chair against his skin. "I, uh, was with Miss Toni Webster," he said, sounding confident. "We were on a date."

A hint of a smile played on Callum's lips. "Interesting. And how long did you know Ms Webster before this date?"

"Not long," Danny admitted. "We met a few days ago."

Callum raised an eyebrow. "I see," was all the detective said.

"I heard you went to a notoriously shady bar on your first date?"

"No, it was not a notoriously shady bar. It was a picnic under the stars."

"Mr Reynolds warned you to be careful of me before you sat down. Perhaps he knows more about your involvement than you are letting on."

Danny's mind raced. Should he deny Abe's words? Or play along? He opted for the former, unsure what consequences either option held.

"Mr Reynolds is mistaken," he said forcefully. "I have nothing to hide."

Callum looked at the bar and noticed that Abe was just sitting there, watching him. Detective Callum stood up and turned to all the guests in the restaurant and the staff.

"Ladies and gentlemen, you may leave now. I might have further questions and if so, I will be in contact with you individually. Thank you for your time this morning."

As soon as the statement sank in everyone's mind, the guests stood up and left the restaurant.

"Samuel, you and Gertie can stay behind, but your staff may go about their normal duties."

Danny opened his mouth to speak, but Detective Callum motioned for Danny not to, so Danny stopped.

After the room was empty but Samuel, Gertie, the detective and Danny Samuel spoke: "The detective had you going for a while, Danny," said Samuel with a smile.

"What? Samuel? Gertie? Did you know this was going to happen? Why did you not tell me?"

"We wanted all the guests in the room to see your expression when I asked you those questions, Mr Monk. Your answers allowed me to observe them as you spoke," responded detective Callum.

Before Danny could respond, the detective said: "Samuel, Gertie, thank you both for your help today. I need some privacy with Mr Monk."

"Of course," and they both leave, leaving just Danny and the detective in the restaurant alone.

Danny takes the offensive approach and asks: "Why did you not want Samuel or Gertie to let me know what was going to happen?

"I have my reasons, Mr Monk, but the truth, like a well-told story, requires not only a setting but also characters who reveal their true selves when the plot thickens."

That answer takes aback Danny, for he has heard it somewhere. Or has he read it? Danny just asked: "Where have I heard that before, Detective Callum?"

A small laugh comes out from Detective Callum and responds: "From one of my favourite fictional detectives, Hercule Poirot."

"Oh, him, I know very well," answered Danny.

"Yes, Mr Monk. I know a lot about you. I did a lot of research on all the guests last night after Samuel called me and I found out some interesting things about several characters here, including you, Mr Monk."

"Really? Pray tell what is so interesting of yours truly?"

"Well, Mr Monk, I had a long conversation with Senior Detective Malcolm Cassell."

Danny's eyebrows shot up, his expression a mixture of intrigue and suspicion. "Senior Detective Cassell, did you say? The detective I helped crack the case of the murdered house servant?"

"The same," Detective Callum said, leaning back confidently. "And let me tell you, Mr Monk, he had quite a lot to say about you."

Danny smiled. "Really? And what did the esteemed Senior Detective Cassell have to say about a simple bookshop owner like me?"

"He merely said that you are not what you seem to profess you are: not a simple bookshop owner."

"Really? Can you elaborate a bit more for me? I am curious as to the conversation you had with Senior Detective Cassell."

"He was...impressed," Callum said, drawing out the word. "Cassell spoke of your keen eye for detail, your unusual timing on settling all outstanding loans, all in cash by the way, but he must admit you have some unorthodox methods that helped him with that case, and how you always seem to be in the graces of powerful and beautiful women."

Danny scoffed. "Flattery will get you nowhere, my friend. What is your angle here?"

Callum chuckled. "No angle, Mr Monk. Just a genuine interest in someone who is in the most interesting moments of life and, because of his eccentricities, or connections, seems to keep the local police force in check."

"Eccentricities, you say?" Danny's voice sharpened. "After all, I did for Senior Detective Cassell was to tidy up his crime scene and handing him the murderer on his lap. He is still looking for something to pin on me. Is that it, Detective Callum?"

"Perhaps," Callum admitted with a grin. "But hey, detectives can be like dogs with a bone. Hard to let go, you know?"

"Yes, I do Detective Callum."

"Now, I would love to hear your take on this watch theft. Senior Detective Cassell mentions you have some...unique insights."

Danny hesitated, his gaze flickering around the room. Finally, he sighed. "Alright, all right. I have an opinion or two on this."

Before Detective Callum could asked, all you hear is: "Danny mi vida, I have arrived."

Albert and his timing. It is always perfect.

Chapter Thirty-Three - Conclusions

Detective Cullum turned and looked at Albert, and Danny thought he heard a small chuckle come out of Detective Cullum.

Albert stands there by the restaurant door looking like a fresh peacock rushing in for a feed. His flamboyant outfit comprises a vibrant purple velvet blazer adorned with golden embroidery, catching the bright morning sunlight. Beneath, a crisp white shirt with ruffled sleeves peeks out, reminiscent of the Victorian era. His trousers, tailored to perfection, boast a daring pinstripe pattern, perfectly complementing his ensemble. To complete the look, Albert dons a pair of polished leather shoes with silver buckles, each step echoing confidence and sophistication. As he strides into the restaurant, in his impeccable and outrageous style, he is a vision of elegance and panache, ready to seize the day, or evening, because you never know what Albert is planning.

"Danny, my darling, I just drove in as I promised and here, I find you with this handsome stranger all by your lonesome. Did I interrupt something?"

Danny's eyes widened in surprise at Albert's sudden appearance, but a mischievous grin played on his lips. "Interrupt? Oh, not at all, Albert," Danny replied, gesturing for Albert to join them.

"Just having a pleasant chat with Liam Callum."

Callum nodded in greeting, a knowing twinkle in his eye as if he sensed the dynamic between Danny and Albert but noticed that Danny did not introduce him as Detective Liam Callum.

Albert chuckled knowingly, sliding into the seat beside Danny. "Well, then, I couldn't miss out on the fun," he remarked, casting a sidelong glance at Danny before turning his attention to Callum.

"Hi there, handsome. My name is Albert Matthew Guzman, and I am Danny's best friend and business partner. Please call me Albert and tell me, Liam Callum, how do you know this troublemaker and is there a Mrs Callum?"

Callum grinned at Albert's teased tone, his eyes sparkling with amusement. "Ah, well, Albert, let's just say Danny here has a knack for getting himself into interesting situations," Liam replied cryptically, sharing a knowing look with Danny. "As for your second question..." He paused, a playful glint in his eyes as he glanced at Albert. "There is indeed a Mrs Callum, though she's much better at keeping me in line than I am at solving mysteries." Detective Callum chuckled; his expression was warm with affection. "But enough about me. What brings you here this morning, Albert? Surely not just to rescue Danny from my interrogations?"

"Interrogations? Are you police?" Albert blurted; his flamboyance momentarily forgotten. The question hung heavy in the air, shattering the tense playfulness, and replacing it with a sharp undercurrent of fear. He stole a glance at Danny, searching for any explanation, any clue what was happening. His own arrival felt sudden and irrelevant, caught amidst this unexpected revelation.

"Allow me to introduce myself. I am Detective Liam Callum of the local constabulary. At your service."

Albert looked at Danny and back at Detective Callum and could not help himself. "What are you accusing my sweet Danny of? Whatever it is, he is innocent. Innocent, I tell you."

Detective Callum raised an eyebrow at Albert's impassioned defence of Danny, a faint smirk playing on his lips.

"Easy there, Albert," he said, holding up a hand in a placated gesture. "No one's accusing anyone of anything just yet."

Detective Callum leaned back in his chair, his expression thoughtful. "But it wouldn't hurt to have a chat, you know, to clear up a few things."

Danny shot Albert a reassuring glance, silently urging him to remain calm. Albert took a deep breath, his protective instincts still on high alert. "Alright, Detective Liam Callum," he said, his voice firm but measured. "But I will keep an eye on you. Danny's my friend, and I will not stand for any unfair treatment. Even from a handsome creature like yourself. "

"I understand Albert. Why are you here today?"

Before Albert could answer, Danny interjected.

"Albert, I want you to know that Detective Cullum and Senior Detective Cassell had a conversation last night about me, and I am sure you both discussed our encounters with Cassell. Am I correct Detective?"

Albert was about to freak out and blurb out something dumb when Detective Callum said: "I understand your concern, Danny," his tone sympathetic. "But sometimes, we have to sift through a lot of noise to get to the truth." He paused, his gaze shifting between Albert and Danny.

"Cassell's accusations may be baseless, but I am here to ensure that everything is open. If you both are indeed innocent, then there is nothing to worry about." His voice carried a note of reassurance, though his eyes held a steely determination. "So, let us have that chat, shall we? And hopefully, we can put this all behind us."

Albert looked at Danny, and Danny just nodded.

"OK, Detective, have your way with me," retorted Albert.

Danny could not help but smile at Albert's approach to the detective, but Detective Callum took Albert's comment in stride.

"My original question Albert. Why are you here today?"

Looking around, albert saw no one around and could not help himself asked: "Is this a serve yourself bar? Can I just get myself a drink?"

"No Albert," Danny stated. "Let us hear detective Callum out and then I will take you for a lynch and some drinks. OK?"

"That sounds wonderful Danny," looking at the detective Albert just said: "OK, let us get this uncomfortable moment out of the way Detective Callum."

For the next twenty minutes, Callum smoothly asked questions of Albert and Danny. Making some cursory notes in his notebook as he noted an answer of interest. Both Albert and

Danny answered all questions with no hesitation, which gave Detective Callum some comfort since it has been his experience that an individual has four diverse ways to answering a question.

When individuals give quick and straightforward answers, detectives can interpret it as a sign of cooperation and honesty. The individual may be forthcoming because they have nothing to hide and want to assist in the investigation. It has been Detective Callum's experience that this is a 50-50 proposition. Some folks are simply good at lying and making it sound so truthful.

If the answers seem overly rehearsed or scripted, it has been detective Callum's experience that quick responses as a sign that the individual was prepared for the interrogation. This did not appear to be the case with either Danny or Albert.

Sometimes, individuals may answer questions quickly because of nervousness or anxiety. Again, neither Danny nor Albert hurried their answers.

Finally, some individuals may try to appear cooperative by providing rapid responses while subtly avoiding or manipulating certain questions to conceal the truth. That was not the case here, concluded the detective.

After making a few more notes, Callum asked Danny,

"Danny, any thoughts on the robbery of Mr Reynold's watch?"

Albert looked curiously at Danny. "Who is this Mr Reynolds Danny?"

"One of the guests. He reported his Tag Heuer Carrera watch stolen to the inn's owners, and they called Detective

Callum last night and the owners, Samuel and Gertie, held a Hercule Poirot meeting this morning before meeting and detective Callum interviewed everyone. The inn owners, the inn's staff and all the guests, me, being the last one, when you waltzed in."

"Danny, how many times do I need to tell you I do not waltz into a room? I simply present myself in the best manner."

"OK Albert. To answer your question Detective Callum, I have a few suspicious but I need to be sure. When I am ready, unless you discover the culprit first, I will be in touch with you."

Detective Callum gets up and looking at Danny and Albert states: "Gentlemen, I leave you for now. Please keep this conversation between us."

Danny and Albert look at each other and wonder what conclusions the detective walked away with.

Chapter Thirty-Four - Bait

Danny and Albert waited until detective Callum was out of the restaurant and albert jumped with questions: "Danny, mi Principe! Detective Liam Cullum seems more intelligent than Senior Detective Cassell. Why is he wasting time with you and now me as suspects in this small watch theft thing?"

"First Albert, it is not a small watch thing. The missing watch is a TAG Heuer Carrera watch is a masterpiece of precision engineering and timeless design and I believe, depending on the watch style, they would retail between $10,000 to $40,000."

"Second, the guest in question, Mr Reynolds, has been quite a character here. He has taken the time to speak with all the staff, asking questions about the guests and having either breakfast or dinner with them and, as one guest stated to me, 'pumping them' for information."

"Third, the inn's staff, frequently have stated that Mr Reynolds seems to come out or going into someone's else's room and stops when he sees them and acts as if old age is affecting his mind, and he is confused as to his room. I will tell you albert Mr Reynold has a rational mind when we spoke. I do not think he has any cognitive issues as he prescribes."

"Fourth, when I first met and sat with him over dinner, I noticed he had on what I think was makeup or concealer. I realise some men do wear makeup," giving Albert a quick look and nod, "but I did not think he was the type. Maybe he was just vain and wanted to look younger."

"I find nothing wrong with men wearing makeup. As a matter of fact, some of us do extremely well using it."

"Of course, Albert, I understand, but you did not let me finish my point."

"Please continue Papi."

"I as well had a feeling someone had been in my room. When I walked around the room, I notice a petal on the floor, and it had a smudge on it. It looked like makeup or a concealer."

"Finally, his past occupation might be another clue."

"What do you mean by that, Danny? What does his past occupation show or give you a clue to make him a suspect?"

"Mr Reynolds used to be an owner of Nullica Security Service which provided your standard residential security services to people's homes, and a few years later, he took over Nullica Locks and Safes when the owner had a heart attack and the family needed to sell in a hurry."

"This makes him a suspect, Danny. I think not. By this count, when I asked you to research car alarms or door security systems, which would also make you a suspect. Right?"

"You are right Albert. That would make me, and you, a suspect, and it did, otherwise Senior Detective Malcolm Cassell would not have been so interested in us in our past schemes."

Albert let Danny's words sink in. He could not deny it. Detective Cassell had a point. Their past financial woes, followed by a sudden surge of wealth that paid off everything in cash, made them prime suspects. The sting of the accusation lingered.

Albert's flashy lifestyle, fuelled by their business, had always masked a more precarious reality. No wonder Cassell saw through their façade and suspected them. Their rapid debt repayment and cash-only ventures, while a testament to their hustle, now cast a long, suspicious shadow they might never fully escape.

"Oh well, what is done, is done," thought Albert as he turned to Danny and asked: "OK Danny, now what?"

"Now we go to lunch, and we set a trap for Mr Reynolds."

"I like the lunch part, but how do we do this trap you mention, Danny?"

"That is easy, Albert."

"Tell me corazón!"

"You are the bait."

Albert's flamboyant, vibrant, purple outfit dimmed a bit when Danny said that.

Chapter Thirty-Five – Going Shopping

"Danny, darling, what do you mean I am the bait?" Danny motioned to Albert to get up from the table.

"Come on Albert. Let's go for a quick drive."

"But I have not checked in. I need to freshen up after my drive here."

"Albert, you drove your Bently here, correct?"

"Yes dear. It is outside. Why?"

"You do not need to freshen up. The Bentley made sure you were as fresh as possible in your drive up here. Now let's go. I have a plan I need to plan and explain to you."

As Danny and Albert are headed out, Danny sees Abe Reynolds at the reception desk, talking with Samuel.

"Perfect. Follow my lead, Albert, and do not overact."

Making a face, Albert simply responds winking at Danny: "But darling, if I don't overact, how will you know how much I truly care?"

"Hi Samuel, Abe. This is my dear friend Albert Matthew Guzman, the owner of the finest hair salon in Sydney. Albert, this is Samuel, one of the inn's owners, and Mr Abe Reynolds, one of the guests."

Albert must have been reading my mind, for he extends his hand gracefully, palm facing slightly downwards, fingers gently extended. As he meets Abe's gaze with a warm smile, he offers his hand with a subtle but confident movement, inviting

Abe to clasp it in his own. With a poised and deliberate gesture, he conveys equal measures of respect and friendliness. Abe takes a quick look at Albert and cannot help but notice his watch and points to it.

"My goodness! Is this a 2022 Rolex Day-Date Yellow Gold Diamond Bezel? It is a horological masterpiece. It is exquisite, and it looks marvellous on your wrist, Mr Guzman."

As if on cue, Albert chimes in.

"This little thing? Darling, I have a small collection which I travel with all the time. You never know what you are going to wear, and you must be ready to coordinate at a moment's notice. That is what my mother always taught me, Mr Reynolds."

"Please call me Abe."

With a big smile on his face, Albert winks at Abe and said: "And you must call me Albert."

"Mr Guzman, you have not checked in and your room is ready. Would you like to check in now? I can have Robert take your suitcases upstairs."

"No need Samuel, I am taking Albert out to lunch at the Seashell Café, and he can check in later. I will help him with the suitcases when we return."

"OK Danny. Mr Guzman, just check in when you return," said Samuel, giving Danny a funny look which Albert noticed but did not react to.

"Abe, always a pleasure to speak with you. Maybe the three of us can do dinner sometime?"

"Sure Danny. You name the place and the time. I would love to hear more about your friend's hair salon. It sounds marvellous."

"It is, indeed, superb Abe. Simply superb," answered Albert once again extending his hand to Reynolds who took it and shook it and Abe almost looked like he was going to bow to Albert and kiss his hand but caught himself.

"See you darling," Albert said as Danny and he walked toward Albert's Bentley.

"Albert, I said for you not to exaggerate with the act."

"I was just being me, Danny. You know sweetness, just wonderful," Albert responded with a cheeky smile.

"Albert, you drive. I will give you directions, but first I need to call Toni to see if she can meet us for lunch at the café."

"Toni? Am I going to meet this lovely Toni?"

"If she can make it, yes, you are."

Danny and Albert get into the 1998 Bentley Mulsanne and Danny gives Albert the name of the place he wants to go to first and the address.

"This does not sound like a place to have lunch, Danny?"

"Just punch it into the GPS and drive. I need to connect with Toni."

"Of course, darling. I love it when you are so domineering," Albert answers with a loud laugh.

As Albert puts in the address into the GPS and starts the car, Danny speed dials Toni.

"Hi there, stranger. I was wondering when you would be calling."

"Toni. I am in a friend's car, driving into Crystal Cove to do a bit of shopping. Can we meet in, say, one hour, at the seashell Café for lunch?"

"Yes, count me in. I can be there in an hour. Who is this friend, anyway?"

"Not only my friend, but my business partner. Albert Matthew Guzman. I think you should meet him, for he is going to help me solve the stolen watch affair at the Poplar Inn."

"He is? Is he a police officer or a detective?"

Danny glances at Albert, who is driving towards Crystal Cove with a smile on his face, oblivious to the conversation and again just reaffirms.

"No Toni. He is the bait."

"The bait? I do not understand."

"That is why you are meeting us for lunch. See you soon?"

"You betcha."

Chapter Thirty-Six – Not a Bad Idea

Albert pulls up in front of the store, turns off his auto, and looks at Danny.

"Danny, darling, we are here. What are we doing in this little electronics store?"

"Albert, we are buying a spy camera to see when you place your watch in your nightstand drawer who comes in to steal it. That is why you are the bait, or rather, your watch is."

Albert quickly moves his left hand close to his chest as if protecting the watch and starts rattling away. "My watch? Oh, no, darling. This watch once belong to my grandfather and was given to me by my grandmother Lucia Martinez Gutierrez Guzman. It is a priceless Patek Philippe Calatrava rose gold wristwatch from the early 1960s. I had it appraised at $52,000.00 just last year. No way I am using this as bait. No, no, no!"

Danny almost starts laughing but holds back and simply looks at Albert.

"Your grandmother gave you the watch?"

"Yes, sweetness she did."

"You are sure we did not acquire this watch during one of our ventures into the acquisition world? Did it not fall into our lap? I do not believe it was your grandmothers. Prove me wrong Albert."

Albert looked at Danny and could not help but smile. "Danny, mi cariño, you got me. It was indeed an acquisition, but darling, it is not just about the watch. Look at this watch. It should have been in my family. This is like a connection to my ancestors. This watch could have belonged to my grandfather, a symbol of his hard work and dedication. I feel I would honour his legacy and preserving a piece of our heritage for future generations had he indeed own the watch before we acquired it. It is more than just a timepiece; it is a treasure with sentimental value beyond measure."

"Albert, you told me your family owns a small banana farm in Columbia. We stole that watch. It never was in your family."

"Danny amor, that is not the point. The point is that we need to handle this situation delicately. I was telling everyone that it did, and I have, as a superb and exquisite artist, both in hair styling and form, come to believe it so. In my mind, this watch truly belonged to my grandfather, and it is a part of my family's history, and the fact that I believe this point so strongly is all that matters. Goodness, my boy, I could pass a lie detector test if I had to and attest to this. I believe it to be so. We must make sure we can retrieve it after your crazy plan."

"Albert, you are going overboard with this. I just need for you to place it in the nightstand drawer. It is bait. It will not leave your room. I will be in my room monitoring it to make sure it does not leave your room."

"Promise, darling. You look out for my grandfather's watch?"

"Your grandfa... Yes, Albert I will look and make sure nothing happens to your grandfather's watch. Now let us go meet Toni. She is also has a part in this plan to play."

"See darling, I even have you convinced it was my grandfather's watch. Ah, I am so good with my scene deliveries. Am I not?"

"Yes. You are perfect. Now wait here while I buy the camera.

It did not take long. The little electronics store in Crystal Cove had a website, and Danny had gone online and found what he needed. Nothing fancy but powerful enough to do what he wanted the camera to do. In less that fifteen minutes, Danny was sitting next to Albert in the car.

"That is it? You did? You bought what you needed? Can I see it?" an excited Albert kept harping at Danny.

Danny did not answer Albert but placed a new address into the Bently's navigation system.

"Drive Albert. Once we get to Toni's, I will show you both what I purchased."

Danny could swear that Albert had a pouting face on him, but all he said was: "You are so mean to me sometimes, Danny. OK, I will wait until we reach your girlfriend's place."

"Toni is not my girlfriend, Albert. Friend, yes, but we have not even discussed taking our relationship to that level."

"You have not discussed it? Are you planning to? Do you need my help? I am exceptionally good at getting people to express their feelings."

"Drive Albert. We should be there in ten minutes. I need some quiet time to think how to approach Toni, explain the part I need her to play, and then Samuel, and finally, how to get Detective Liam Callum involved."

"Oh, I like that Detective Liam Callum. He is a cutie."

"Albert, quiet, just drive and let me think."

"I love it when you are forceful. I will be good now and I will be quiet as a mouse and as unassuming as a whisper,"

Danny gives Albert a look and Albert focuses on his driving fully now.

Arriving at Toni's, Danny has formulated his plan and is sure it will work. All he had to do was share it with Toni and let her take the lead.

Danny knocks on Toni's door, and she opens it with the biggest smile Danny has seen and it fills him. As always, Toni's attire radiates a summery aura, as she elegantly dons a light off-the-shoulder dress. The dress, with its off-the-shoulder design, accentuates her collarbones and shoulders, lending a touch of allure to her ensemble.

The fabric flows freely with her movements, catching the light with each movement she makes, creating an ethereal and effortless charm.

Toni complements the dress perfectly with a minimal accessory, such as a dainty necklace, allowing the dress to remain the focal point of her outfit. Her hair, swept back in loose waves, adds a carefree yet chic vibe to her overall look.

"She is plainly adorable," thought Danny as he reaches for her hand, but Albert jumped in between them.

"This is the Toni you have been speaking about so eloquently to me these past few days, Danny. She is so lovely. Look at that hair. She does not need any professional help. She is perfect, just perfect, my boy. How lucky you are to find such a gem in this quaint little hamlet!"

"Toni, this is Albert Matthew Guzman, my best friend, and business partner. Albert, this is Toni Webster, my friend."

"Come on Danny, your friend? No, that is not how you described Toni to me. You said she is an enchantress weaving her spell upon you, drawing you into her world with every word and gesture, and you are loving it."

Danny was dumbstruck. As always, Albert leaps in with both feet, not worrying about what he says or to whom he says it. How was Toni going to react to this last statement from him?

"My, ooh, me. I am now an enchantress weaving my spell upon you, drawing you into my world with every word and gesture I say and do, and you are loving it. Is that right, Danny? Are you loving it?"

"Well, yes, of course I am Toni, but listen, can we come in? I need to go over something with you that I need you to do to help me setup the potential thief of Mr Reynold's watch."

"Of course, please come in gentlemen," as Toni waves them in.

As Danny follows Albert into Toni's home, he can only think that his relationship with Toni is being accelerated faster than he had in mind, and maybe it was not a bad idea.

Chapter Thirty-Seven – Bawling Like a Baby

Albert walks in first and after taking a few steps, turns around and exclaimed: "Toni, sweetheart, what an adorable place you have. Did you do the decorating yourself or did you hire someone? This place is just marvellous. A feast to the eyes."

"I would love to take full credit, but I can only take partial credit, Albert. I did hire both an architect and an interior designer, but a lot of what you see were my ideas, just professionally displayed."

"Darling, you are so honest. I love that about you. You could have told me a porky and I would not hesitate in believing you."

"That is not who I am. I am always for one hundred per cent honesty."

Albert gives Danny a quick glance and nods as if to said, *"See, you need to tell her everything, Danny boy. Soon."*

"OK, now enough of this dual adoration, you two. I need to go over my idea. Here, let me show you what I purchased that will help us catch the thief."

Opening the bag from the electronics store, Danny brings out a smoke detector.

"Sweetie. Is this what you bought at the electronics store? You bought a smoke detector?"

"No, it is a dummy smoke detector Wi-Fi spy camera. It is a high definition and can perform many powerful functions, such as a remote viewing of live video, PIR human body sensing, motion detection, high definition video recording, and has automatic night vision."

"So, you are going to place it where Danny?" asked Toni.

Danny grabs Albert's hand and shows Toni the watch Albert is wearing.

Toni makes a funny face as if to understand and then the light bulb goes off.

"This is an exquisite watch, Danny. Are you proposing that Albert just leaves it in his room, easily accessible, so whomever stole Mr Reynold's watch can take this one as well?

"Yes, and no. I do not want to make it too obvious for the thief might get suspicious, but this is where you come into this play."

"Me? What do I need to do?"

"I need you to make a big deal of this watch tomorrow morning during breakfast when Albert is sitting with Mr Reynolds at their table."

"Tomorrow morning? What would I be doing there in the morning? I have taken these days off to spend with you."

Danny smiled and let out a small chuckle.

"Toni, you are not going to be working you are coming to pick me and Albert for a day outing on the ocean. You are then going to make a big deal of this watch in front of Mr Reynolds and Albert will go into his performance as to the history of the watch and the value of the watch. Then after Albert finishes his story, which I hope will not be long, he will make sure he mentions that he does not trust hotel safes and he normally just tucks his valuables on a nightstand under something, a book, or a handkerchief and he has never had any issues."

"Danny mi bombón. Why my watch? Why not yours? It is just as nice?"

"Albert, we have gone through this already. Your watch is something I believe the thief will jump at when he sees it on your wrist."

"Danny, you sound like you know who the thief is? Do you?" asked Toni.

"I have a strong inclination, but this dummy smoke detector will capture everything while we are gone on our ocean trip."

"Darling, if we are on a boat somewhere in the ocean, how do we stop the thief from running away with my watch?"

"Simple. We enlist the help of Samuel and Gertie and the expertise of detective Liam Callum however they will be needed a bit later. I do not believe the thief will take Albert's watch and run out of the Poplar Inn right away."

"So, you are bringing in them into this setup as well. Danny, if you know, why not just tell us and the detective and let him oversee it?" asked Toni.

"Toni, before I tell you why I am bringing Samuel, Gertie, and the detective into this trap, there are a few things I need to share with you if our current situation is to grow into something more serious."

"Grow more serious? What are you saying Danny?" a surprised Toni states.

"That is my cue to step away," said Albert, but Danny grabbed his arm and yanked him down back in his seat.

"No Albert, you need to stay here, for you are also part of the story and Toni needs to know everything."

Albert said: "Everything," in a shaky voice, but sits there quietly.

"Yes, she needs to know everything. Let me start from the beginning...."

Toni heard Danny explained how he and Albert had met and started their side 'acquisition business', which was just larceny on a large scale. As Danny's voice detail their first meeting, and how Albert helped Danny get into the bookstore business, Toni could not help but feel a mixture of intrigue and unease. She had known Danny for just a few weeks, but this revelation about his illicit activities with Albert shed new light on his character.

Sitting across from Danny, Toni observed his animated gestures and the gleam in his eyes as he recounted the beginnings of their enterprise. According to him, it all started innocently enough—a few small-time schemes here and there to make ends meet since as he said: "Retail is a hard business to make a profit." But as they tasted success, their ambitions grew, leading them deeper into the world of crime. Toni could not shake off the realisation that she had been oblivious to this side of Danny's life, and she could not help but wonder how deep he had been incredibly involved.

As Danny delved into the intricate details of their operations, Toni's mind raced with conflicting thoughts. On one hand, she was fascinated by the audacity and cunning displayed by Danny and Albert in their criminal endeavours. On the other hand, she could not shake the moral dilemma gnawing at her conscience. She had always prided herself on her integrity and adherence to the law, but now she found herself uncomfortably close to individuals who lived on the other side of it. As the story wore on, Toni grappled with the weight of what she had learned, unsure of where her loyalty lay and what actions she should take next when Danny just stopped his story and said to her: "Toni, I am so sorry I never shared this with you before but I have grown so fond of you that I just could not go on not letting you know for I did not want you to get too attached and then I break your heart. I can assure you that both Albert and I are no longer in the acquisition business."

Albert was sniffing a little and had taken out his monogram handkerchief and was letting the handkerchief absorb one or two tears that came out of his eyes.

Toni just sits there quietly pondering what she just heard. Despite the unsettling revelation of Albert's and Danny's past criminal activities, Toni found herself torn by conflicting emotions. While her sense of morality urged her to distance herself from such an individual who had such illicit dealings, her love for Danny ran deep, clouding her judgement with an unwavering loyalty. As she gazed into his eyes, she saw more than just a man with a troubled past; she saw the person she loved, flaws and all. Despite the risks and uncertainties, Toni resolved to stand by Danny, choosing to believe in the possibility of redemption and a future untainted by his shady past. With a mixture of trepidation and unwavering devotion, she took Danny's hand and asked.

"These activities you mentioned have stopped?"

"Yes ma'am," answered Albert and quickly realising it was not him she was asked the question.

Danny began, his voice steady yet tinged with vulnerability, "Toni, I know my past is filled with mistakes and regrets, but I swear to you, those days are behind me now. All I want to say to you is that this past life is behind me and Albert, and I want to start with you by my side. You are my light, and I am through living with this dark past. I want to build something real, something we can be proud of together, and I am ready to prove it to you every single day."

As he spoke, Toni felt a surge of hope and reassurance wash over her. But Danny did not know everything about her for she had not shared a terrible event from her past. Toni felt confused. Was it love or attraction? If it were love, she felt maybe, just maybe, that love could just conquer the shadows of their past.

As if on cue, Albert filled with emotion started bawling like a baby.

Chapter Thirty-Eight – The Three Musketeers

Albert kept bawling like a two-month-old, wanting to be fed Danny, went up to him and, taking one of the lounge pillows, whacked him over the head.

"Danny mi corazón, why did you do that? Do you not see that these are tears of joy?"

As Toni sat watching Danny and Albert's interaction, her mind swirled with conflicting emotions. She had always considered that her relationship with Danny might grow into something special and he just told her he wants to build something together.

She replayed their moments together in her mind. She realised that her feelings for him ran deeper than mere friendship. It was a realisation that both excited and terrified her. How could she get involved with such a man? A criminal. Has he or Albert or both been to prison? Do they have any more baggage? More importantly, now that she knew, what was she supposed to do about it?

The more Toni dwelled on her newfound feelings for Danny, the more she understood the significance of them. It wasn't just a passing infatuation or a fleeting crush. It was something profound, something that had been growing silently within her during these days. The time spent together has been special, almost magical. Could such a thing like love move that fast? Was it love or attraction? Danny said he wanted to build something together. Did she feel the same towards him?

Yes, she has fallen for this complicated man. She could not ignore it any longer. But along with the realisation of her love for him came another truth she had been keeping buried deep within herself—a secret she knew she had to share with him, no matter the consequences. It weighed heavily on her heart, threatening to consume her if she did not find the courage to speak up.

Suddenly, Toni got up and started pacing back and forth, rehearsing the words she wanted to say to Danny. She felt a sense of vulnerability wash over her. She noticed this caused both Danny and Albert to stop their bickering and that watched her paced.

Speaking about her feelings was one thing, but revealing her secret was an entirely different challenge. She feared how he might react, whether he would still see her in the same light afterward. But she knew she could not continue hiding this part of herself from him. If their friendship, their new blossoming romantic relationship, meant anything to them, she had to be honest, even if it meant risking everything.

With a deep breath, Toni makes her decision. She would tell Danny the truth, no matter how difficult it might be. She could not keep denying her feelings for him, nor could she continue carrying the weight of her secret alone. As nervous as she was about his reaction, she knew that honesty was the only path forward. Whatever happened next, she would face it with courage and hope, knowing that she could not truly move forward until she had laid her heart bare before him.

Toni's heart raced as she sat again on the lounge with Danny, her mind grappling with the weight of the secret she was about to reveal. She had never spoken of this to anyone, not even her mother, but she knew she could not keep it buried any longer. Taking a shaky breath, she met Danny's gaze, steeling herself for his reaction. "Danny," she began, her voice trembling with emotion, "there's something I need to tell you, something I've kept hidden for years." Danny's brow furrowed with concern as he leaned in closer, silently urged her to continued. "When I was a teenager," Toni continued, her voice barely above a whisper, "I... I killed my stepfather."

The words hung heavy in the air as Toni watched Danny's expression shift from confusion to shock. He opened his mouth to speak, but no words came out, his mind struggling to comprehend the enormity of what she had just confessed. Toni pressed on, her voice steady now as she recounted the events of that fateful night, the fear, and desperation that had driven her to take such drastic action. She explained how her stepfather had been abusive, how she and her mother had endured his cruelty for years, until one night, when he was beating her, she had snapped, unable to bear it any longer, and stabbed him with a kitchen knife.

Toni explained that everything happen so quickly that she had not even realised she had picked up the knife and thrusted it into his heart. He collapsed and died right there on the kitchen floor.

As soon as she grasped what she had done, she called her mother to come from the café and when Cecilia came, detailed what had happened.

The pair decided that they would take the body and dump it in Whispering Pines Lake after weighting the body down and to this day the body had not been found. If anyone ever asked Cecilia and Toni would simply say he had stormed out and left them.

As Toni finished her confession, she braced herself for Danny's reaction, unsure of how he would respond to such a revelation. But to her surprise, there was no judgement in his eyes, only a deep sadness and compassion. Without a word, he reached out to take her hand in his, offering her the silent support she so desperately needed at that moment. Toni looked into his eyes. She knew that she had made the right decision to confide in him, that she was no longer alone in carrying the burden of her past.

Albert quickly came over and hugged Toni.

"Mija, you have been carrying this burden all these years. I, for one, know about secrets and while I am not about to share them here, I am so glad you have shared yours with us. It will remain between us. Right Danny?"

Danny, still holding Toni's hand, simply nodded in agreement with Albert's statement, silently conveying his unwavering support for Toni.

"So, this does not change anything, Danny?" Toni asked.

"Not a thing except that my feelings for you are even more for you sharing this secret with me, with us."

"We are now the three musketeers," exclaimed Albert as he gets up and starts swinging an air sword in the air around the room.

Danny couldn't believe his ears when Albert casually mentioned taking Toni's confession to a murder, as if it were just a plot twist in a Three Musketeers reboot, complete with swashbuckling self-defence moves and his prancing around the room.

"This is serious, Albert, and besides, there were four musketeers in Alexandre Dumas's story," explained Danny.

"I know, but Toni's mother is not here, so here we are only the three."

Toni observed the banter between Danny and Albert, with Albert incredulously comparing their situation to the escapades of the Three Musketeers. She could not help but burst into laughter. It dawned on her that this bizarre exchange was more than just a humorous moment; it was a sign of true trust. In that laughter filled moment, Toni realised that they were truly bonded to each other, sharing secrets, and forming a tie that transcended the ordinary. It was not just about the confession anymore; it was about the connection forged through shared laughter and absurdity, a bond worthy of even the most adventurous musketeers.

Chapter Thirty-Nine – Broadway Song

Albert stopped twirling around with his pretend air sword and plunked himself on the lounge.

"I am exhausted after all this. Is there a bar in this joint?" winking at Toni.

Toni now more relaxed that ever motions towards the kitchen.

"Am I supposed to get my own drinks? Service has gone down the gurgler."

As Albert heads into the kitchen, Danny looks at Toni and just says: "I love you Antonia 'Toni' Webster."

With a big smile of relief on her face Toni had a fun response: "Ditto, Mr Monk," and gives him a long kiss.

Walking in with a pitcher and three wine glasses, Albert comments: "Get a room, you two. There is much to do still, right, Danny?"

"Indeed, my trusted friend. Let me share my plan and how each of you will have an intricate part to play, as well as Samuel and Gertie and later our detective friend, but first, what did you bring in that pitcher?"

"Sangria, my own concoction, my darling. I took some of Toni's fruits that were on the kitchen counter, such as apples and oranges, and added plenty of sugar into the pitcher. I took some orange juice from the fridge and found that wonderful brandy you love so much, you know, Harvey Bristol Cream, and threw it in for good measure and finally, I found a wonderful red wine and just stirred it to incorporate the different flavours and 'ta-da' a perfect sangria."

Albert poured us each a glass and indeed he had done himself well.

"What is my part in this Daniel Monk production of *To Catch a Thief*?" said Toni, wetting her lips on the sangria.

Danny spent the next thirty minutes explaining what Toni and Albert needed to do in the morning over breakfast and after a few excruciating questions from Albert.

"What should I wear?"

"Is there a tone I need to have?"

"What is my motivation for the scene?"

It all fell into place just as the last glass of sangria was being filled. Danny looked at his watch. It was 7:30PM plenty of time to make the calls.

"OK, now that we know your part. We need to get ready for our ocean sail and I need to get in touch with Samuel and fill him in on his own participation in the morning as well as Gertie's, if all goes as I envisioned."

The sangria had started to work its magic on Albert, who started singing *We Sail the Ocean Blue* from HMS Pinafore with a slur and dancing to boot.

"No more for you Albert, let's go."

"Where are we going, sweetie?"

"To the Poplar Inn. You need to sleep it off. You can handle drink well. What happen here? Why is this sangria affecting you so much?"

"Don't know, and I don't care. I feel wonderful as a matter of fact," and off again into a song this time *I Feel Pretty* from West Side Story.

"Give me the keys to the Bentley. I will drive and you start sleeping in the back sit."

"Yes, mon capitaine," slurred Albert.

"Do you want me to come with you?" asked Toni.

"No, stay, clean up, and I will see you early in the morning. Maybe a little earlier to make sure Albert is ready for his part, OK?"

"OK, I will get there a bit earlier and make sure he is ready. I will make sure he is ready for his performance as I walk in with him into the dining area. You will be there as well, correct?"

"You got him down already, Toni, and yes, I will be in the room already when you get there as well to make sure he is ready. After you leave, I will position the camera and walk in afterwards into the dining area myself and join you both at Abe's table if all goes as planned."

"Sounds like a plan Danny and yes, he is easy to understand, just like you," and gives Danny a kiss.

Albert seems oblivious to the conversation and just smiles as Danny turns and grabs him and, as they head down to the car, Albert starts a new Broadway song.

Chapter Forty – Irish Coffee

Since it was early, I used the Bentley's phone system to dial up the Poplar Inn and got Gertie and asked her to get Samuel and call me back when they are both together so they can put me on speakerphone. Gertie hung up and five minutes later, called back.

"What's up Danny?" asked Samuel.

"I have an idea on who the thief is that took Mr Reynold's watch and I have a plan to catch them at their next activity."

"If you know Danny, why not tell detective Callum and let him handle it," interjected Gertie.

"I need to rephrase my statement. I have a strong suspicion who the thief is, and I have no proof, but with your help we will get the proof. Are you guys available for a thirty-minute chat in about fifteen minutes? Mr Guzman and I are on the way back to the inn from Toni's."

Danny waited a few seconds and then Samuel said: "We will be ready to speak with you both when you get here. I will make sure we have privacy in our office."

"Excellent. See you soon," and Danny pushes the disconnect button on the dashboard screen.

"Do you think you can pull this off, Danny? I mean, my watch is at stake here. What if I lose it?"

Danny looks at Albert and thinks to himself: *"well, you did not worry when we stole it in the first place,"* but said: "I am one hundred per cent sure this plan will work with both you and Toni doing your part and Samuel and Gertie doing theirs."

"I hope so, darling. I worry so much."

Just then Danny pulls into the inn's car park, shuts the Bently off and they walk into the inn. Immediately, they see both Samuel and Gertie behind the counter and walk over.

"Danny, Mr Guzman, follow me into the office. I will let Gertie call Robert so he can watch the reception desk and then she will join us."

As Danny and Albert are led into the inn's office, a sense of warmth and comfort envelops them. The room is cosy yet well-organised, with an inviting atmosphere that immediately puts visitors at ease.

Rustic decorations such as framed photographs of scenic landscapes or quaint paintings of Crystal Cove's village life adorn the walls, adding to the charm of the space. Soft ambient lighting casts a gentle glow, creating a soothing ambiance.

Guests can relax and wait or converse with the innkeeper in the cosy seating area, which is furnished with plush armchairs and a wooden table.

In the centre of the room stands a sturdy wooden desk, its surface arranged with papers, pens and a vintage ledger book. Shelves line the walls, filled with books, trinkets and various knick-knacks, each telling a story of the inn's history and the travellers who have passed through its doors. A small pot of freshly brewed coffee emits a comforting aroma, and Samuel invites Danny and Albert to sit to indulge in a warm beverage.

"Boys, how about a cuppa?" said Samuel as he gestures towards the seating area.

"I will indulge in a coffee, Mr Bailey, if it is an Irish coffee?" states Albert.

"Please call me Samuel and yes, I can indulge you with one. I just enjoy those as well, so I have all the ingredients handy. How about you Danny?"

"I am good Samuel. You go ahead."

Samuel walks over to the small fridge in the corner, which also includes a small area that includes a sink and takes out whipped heavy cream. Samuel starts the kettle and when it hits the boil, pours the hot water into two mugs to preheat it and then pours the hot water out of the mugs. Taking the same kettle, he pours the piping hot coffee into the warmed mugs glass until they are about three-fourths full. Samuel then adds brown sugar and stirs until the sugar completely dissolves. Opening a fresh bottle of Irish whiskey, he pours that in and tops both mugs with the whipped heavy cream by pouring gently over the back of the spoon. *The smell is out of this world*, thought Danny, thinking he should have said yes to the offer.

Just then, in walks in Gertie.

"Samuel Bailey, already hitting the grog?"

"Now sweetheart, I offered it to the gentlemen here, and how could I not join them? You have always said to me that a good innkeeper needs to make sure the guests are taking care of, so here I am, taking care. Besides, I did not think you would want to partake in a drink this late at night. You usually do not, so I did not ask."

"Then, keep going and make me one, since I believe Danny has quite a story to share with us."

"Indeed, I do Gertie. Mind if I start Samuel as you prepare Gertie's coffee?"

"Please go ahead. I can multitask," he said with a big smile on his face to which Gertie just grunted and mumbled: "As if."

So, while Samuel prepared Gertie's coffee, Danny began expressing his thoughts and suspicions to Samuel and Gertie regarding the identity of the thief, outlining a plan to lure the culprit out and finally nail them with concrete evidence. He emphasised the necessity for their involvement, stressing that their contributions were crucial to catching the thief red-handed. After finishing, Gertie spoke first.

"Danny, you have thought this through well and I understand why you do not wish to bring in detective Callum just yet but at the appropriate time." Looking at Samuel, Gertie continued: "Samuel, you are the worst liar I ever seen. Will you be able to carry your part? This plan hinges on your ability to be quite an impressive actor?"

Looking flush, Samuel answers Gertie with, "Hey! I can be subtle! Remember that time I convinced Mrs Higgins I was allergic to marigolds to avoid weeding the garden all summer? It was a horrendously sweltering summer. I should have received an Australian Academy of Cinema and Television Arts award for that performance?"

Gertie nodded and looking at both Danny and albert just said: "He was good that day. By the way, Mr Reynolds told me he was checking out the day after tomorrow. Will we have time to implement this plan, Danny?"

"Actually, this works in our favour. If all of you do your part in the morning, this will work like a charm."

"I am ready, sweetie. Just let me face my audience," said Albert.

"Excellent. Then everyone knows their part. It is getting late so I am off to bed," and looking at Albert Danny states: "You should too Albert."

"One more coffee please, they are delicious," and he holds the mug towards Samuel.

"No," he grabs Albert and lifts him from the cosy chair, as Danny bids good night to the Baileys Samuel told Danny to wait.

Samuel reaches into his desk and gets a key, and hands it to Danny.

"He is my master key. It will get you into any of the rooms."

"Thanks Samuel, Gertie. You both have a good night," and then he guides albert out the office door towards the stairs.

Samuel and Gertie remain in their office, still enjoying their own coffee, and Gertie remarks, "You know what, Samuel?"

"What darling?"

"Who do those two remind you of?"

"No idea. Who do you reckon?"

"Those two remind me of husband and wife the way they handle themselves."

"You know, I also have the same impression," Samuel added as he takes his last sip of his Irish coffee.

Chapter Forty-One – Not a Bad Holiday Trip

Abe Reynolds has always been an early riser. There has not been one day where he has slept in to 7 AM. He is up at 5 AM every day, no matter what time he goes to bed. Abe never worried about his stamina because he has been blessed with a stamina that should be in the body of a thirty-five-year-old, not a seventy-four-year-old male like him, because of lack of sleep.

Getting up, he goes into the toilet and does his morning routine and brushes his teeth before coming back out and starting the kettle. The Poplar Inn had a nice electric kettle which he enjoyed using more than he thought since his place he has the old-style kettle which needs to be heated on his gas stove. *"It's time I upgrade,"* he said to himself with a smile.

And so, he should.

When he gets back home, he will complete the insurance report on his 'stolen' watch and put in a claim. He always was a smart biscuit, his old mum used to say. When Abe came upon his stolen TAG Heuer Carrera watch at the first hotel, he stayed in on his first trip after retiring.

The previous owner had been an obnoxious and heavily intoxicated old buffoon who had purchased the watch in an all cash transaction and shared with him that fact over drinks one night and even boasted the jeweller had provided him with a cash receipt. That in itself was nothing until he dropped a bomb of a statement on Abe. Abe remembers the conversation exactly as it had happened yesterday.

"Abe, do you know how much this watch cost me?" sliding the cash receipt on the table towards Abe. Before Abe could look at the receipt, the drunk said: "Zero. Nada, Nil. Nothing."

Abe remembered that when he looked at the receipt, it showed the sale was for $30,000 and, with a surprised look on his face, questioned the man.

"It says here you purchased it for $30,000. Why are you saying it did not cost you anything? I am confused."

"Because, my dear man, I am going to report it stolen and collect the insurance payment. Piece of cake."

Abe had been retired since selling his security monitoring system and, other than a few small fudges on his tax returns over the years, he had committed nothing as larcenous as what this man had told him in his inebriated state.

"What if you get caught?" asked Abe.

Taking the receipt back and a large gulp of his drink, he answered Abe after letting off a large laugh. "Not going to happen. I did this and many other little transactions over the years and the insurance companies have never suspected me." And with that, he gets up and stumbles out to his room, leaving Abe in total amazement at what had transpired.

The electric kettle makes its announcement with that boiling noise, letting Abe know the water has reached its peak point and it is ready to be poured. Grabbing a mug, Abe pours himself a packet of Moccona French roast provided by the inn, adds two teaspoons of sugar and heads to the window.

The Nautical Nook faces Shore Drive and Abe stands there watching a few of the residents of Crystal Cove head off to work or as the dawn lifts and the mist slowly dissipates.

Abe never thought that the conversation would lead him down the path his life has taken these past few years, and they have been excellent years.

After the idiot had left him alone that night years ago, Abe never thought about what he would do while in retirement. He wanted to travel around Australia and abroad, but his superannuation had limits, so he needed to budget his funds to do his goal of travelling but what if he used his previous experience in both the security and locksmith industry and put them to work once more.

Abe sat there and ordered himself another drink and waited for another hour and thought, what if? What if he took a gamble and expanded his fortune a little by doing something he had never done before? He made the decision that night that if he wanted to really enjoy his retirement and not worry about funds; he needed to acquire more money and what best way to do that than using the skills he used to protect his clients over the years and use them to his advantage.

With that, Abe added the drink to his tab and took the lift. Making sure there were no hall cameras, he found the room where his drinking companion was staying in. and without hesitation, Abe reached into his pocket and took out a small and simple lock pick set he always carries out of habit and in a moment, he entered the room, found the watch and receipt on the nightstand next to the snoring drunk, took them and left the room locking it back up as if nothing ever happen.

The exhilaration he felt almost brought tears to his eyes. He was in heaven.

At that moment, he decided that this was something he was going to do from now on, but making sure he was not too greedy when doing it. He always took one and maybe two articles in the hotels he was staying in and made sure he targets the right individuals with the right articles that can easily be disposed of.

Looking at his watch, he saw the time was almost 7AM and that he should start getting ready for breakfast. He had already mentioned to the innkeepers his intention of leaving the next day, so maybe one more day trip around the area and then he returns home with a $30,000 insurance claim.

"Not a bad holiday trip," Abe thought as he placed the mug on the window ledge and went to the bathroom to get ready.

Chapter Forty-Two - Decision

Danny was never an early riser, but this morning his mind was in high gear and at 5:30AM his eyes bolted open. He did not mind since he needed to be ready by 8AM sharp since, according to Gertie, that is the time when Abe Reynolds always arrived for breakfast.

The plan was simple.

As soon as Gertie sees Abe walking down the stairs for breakfast, she was about to ring Danny who then would go and knock on Albert's room, hoping to find Albert ready and Toni with him. Toni was to make sure Albert left the watch in the nightstand drawer as planned and then they both would go downstairs.

It was then Danny's turn to place the tiny camera in a position in Albert's room that would focus its lens on the nightstand, showing the thief reaching into the drawer and withdrawing the watch.

"Simple plan," thought Danny, but he knew that sometimes simple might not cut it, but it was the best they could without raising suspicion.

He had plenty of time, so Danny sat by his window and just watch the sunrise come up on Crystal Cove. His time here was supposed to be a retreat, a recovery period from Alesia to decide what had happened and clear his mind so he can focus on his future, his business and what life might bring for him in Northport.

Instead, Toni Webster happened.

As he thought about what might happen after all this scheming to catch a thief, he felt Toni would be ready for a more serious relationship, but what if he again he had misread the situation?

"No, I have not read the situation wrong. I think we got a thing going here. Don't we?" Danny said aloud, as if that would cement the statement true. Danny remembers distinctly telling Toni when she shared her secret with him and Albert that his feelings were even more for her after she had shared her secret with him.

But he wondered: *"Did he ever say he loved her?"*

No, he had not told Toni he loved her. But today, after he was able to prove that Abe was the lying about his watch being stolen and catch him in the act of stealing Albert's watch, he would share his feelings for her. With a newfound sense of certainty, he would face Toni and with his heart pounding with nervous anticipation, he will shout out to her those three words: "I love you."

Chapter Forty-Three – What To Do About Danny?

It was 4 AM and Toni did not sleep well last night: her mind was on fire. Yes, she was excited about catching the thief and being a part of the plan to do so with Danny, Albert and the Baileys, but that was not the reason for her insomnia.

It was that damn Daniel Monk.

Ever since he walked into the Seashell Café weeks ago and ordered lunch, she could not keep her mind on nothing else but him.

Those times together at the lake, the many talks and then, when he and Albert shared their past with her, topped it all.

Toni did the unexplained at that moment. She also shared her darkest secret to them, and nothing happen. Danny just cradled her hand, offering much needed support.

Toni also had no reaction when she heard that Danny and Albert were, well criminals, *"Let me clarify,"* she said to herself, *"not criminals but fortunate and elusive acquirers of articles,"* she giggled when she said that but still she knew they were criminals but not as bad as she was for she had committed a murder and so far got away with it, thanks to the help from her mother.

She knew then, at that moment, that she loved him but said nothing, but then neither did he.

All she heard was Danny say was that sharing her secret with him meant more to him, but he never said he loved her, did he?

Toni looked at her watch. 6:40 AM, she had spent so many hours going over her past few weeks with Danny that time just flew, and she needed to get up and get ready to be with Albert to escort him downstairs for breakfast as planned.

"What to do about Danny?" she thought.

She knew she needed to tell Danny she loved him. The words had been simmering just beneath the surface for weeks, a constant warmth in her chest whenever they were together. Laughter lines crinkled the corners of his eyes as he told a story, and a nervous flutter bloomed in her stomach. She yearned for a future painted in shared dreams and whispered secrets, but the fear of rejection gnawed at her. Taking a deep breath, she steeled herself. Today, after the exposure of the thief, she would break the silence, hoping his heart echoed the frantic rhythm of her own.

Chapter Forty-Four – Action

The alarm went off at 6 AM sharp and Albert woke up refreshed and relaxed. He has always enjoyed a glass or two of liquor, but yesterday's Irish Whisky packed a punch, and he went out like a light as soon as he got into his bed.

He remembers Danny grabbing him and dragging him upstairs, opening the door and said something or other like: "Albert, you better be ready by the time Toni gets here at 7:45 AM or else you will hear from me in the morning!"

"Danny can be so macho sometimes and that is why I love him so much," he thought as he fell into the bed until the alarm woke him up. Thank goodness that his practice is always to set the alarm for 6 AM, no matter where he is at home or away.

Standing up, he feels his throat dry and wonders into the bathroom and turn on the light and frightens himself at his vision in the mirror.

"Ghastly, I look horrible, and I need to be at my best this morning for my part in this scheme to catch the thief," he said aloud as he turns on the shower and undressed throwing all his clothes on the floor without a care in the world.

The hot water did the trick and albert towels himself down and, using a spare towel, cleans the foggy mirror and looks at himself.

"Nice, my boy. You look marvellous. Now a touch up here and there and you will be ready for your performance," he thought, smiled, knowing that his part was the most important one.

As Albert gets ready, his mind remembers when he first met Danny. A young man learning the book retail business from old man Hebert McCullum, the then owner of McCullum Booksellers in Northport.

A wave of pure happiness washed over Danny as he enthusiastically accepted his position as McCullum's part-time retail salesperson, shelf stocker and general all-rounder. This newfound calling led him to abandon his studies in architecture and pursue a bachelor's degree in fine arts instead. Later, he took his inheritance from the sale of his parents' home, the little savings he had and applied and received a bank loan to buy McCullum's building, store and inventory and got into the retail business with hope and illusions of success.

Then reality set in.

Retail is a tough business and Albert took pity on him and asked him to take part in his acquisition business.

At Danny was taken aback, but after the first 'acquisition' he started learning more and more and with albert's connections and Danny's youth, they soon were doing 'acquisition jobs' throughout all of Sydney.

The police, of course, were suspicious, *"especially that nasty detective Cassell"*, thought Albert. He finished placing his touch up powder on his neck but no apprehension or arrests and after the fiasco with Alessia both Danny and Albert 'retired' from this side business with a nice nest egg, a few other side, and legal businesses, to supplement their income.

It was time to put on his clothes and Albert came prepared for any occasion and he brought a delicious outfit which he thought would fit the scenario.

Albert's selection is a suit that screams 'summer' with its vibrant hues and flamboyant design. The jacket is crafted from a lightweight seersucker fabric, ensuring comfort even in the heat. The base colour is coral, reminiscent of tropical waters. Adding some flair to the jacket I adorned with bold floral patterns showing oversized blooms in shades of magenta, tangerine and lemon yellow. These patterns cascade down the lapels and across the chest, creating a lively and eye-catching ensemble.

The trousers complement the jacket with a solid white colour to balance out the exuberance of the jacket. Albert could not resist but to tie the look together by accessorising with a vibrant pocket square in a complementary teal pattern featuring geometric shapes in the same vivid colours.

One more touch was the pair of suede loafers in a bold electric blue colour with one or two light yellow streaks, as if rays of sunshine fell upon them.

The finishing flourish came as he nestled a pair of "Aurora Luxe" sunglasses, crafted by the esteemed luxury brand Celestial Eyewear, into his styled hair. Each frame is handcrafted from premium materials like polished titanium, ensuring both resilience and a sumptuous tactile experience. Meanwhile, the lenses boast exceptional quality, crafted from top-tier polarised glass to provide unmatched clarity and shield against harmful UV rays. Adorning the temples are understated yet distinctive embellishments—perhaps the Celestial Eyewear logo etched in

24-karat gold or adorned with glistening Swarovski crystals, underscoring the brand's storied legacy and meticulous craftsmanship.

"Hollywood, here I come. I am ready to turn heads and bring a burst of sunshine wherever I go today!" Albert said, looking at himself just as there was a knock on his door and looking at his 'grandfather's watch' and he sees the time: 7:45 AM.

With a smile on his face Albert opening the door he whispered: "Action" and sees Toni smiled back at him ready for her co-performance of the day.

Chapter Forty-Five – All Set

At 7:55 AM, Abe Reynolds exits his room, makes sure his door is closed, and heads downstairs for breakfast. As he is stepping off the last step of the stairs to head to the dining area, he hears Gertie call out to him: "Mr Reynolds, a moment please," and Abe smiles and heads toward the reception area.

On cue, Samuel moves away from the reception desk and heads to the office and pretends to close the door but leaves it ajar so he can see Mr Reynolds as Gertie queries him. Samuel dials a number and after one ring he says: "He is downstairs at the reception desk now," and hangs up and heads toward the dining area.

After one ring, Danny picks up his mobile, hears Samuel speak and after he hears the dial tone go dead Danny picks up his room keys, the small camera and heads toward his room door, opening it and he exists.

Walking towards albert's room Danny knocks on Albert's room and Toni smiles: "Hi handsome." And Danny reciprocates with a small kiss on her cheek as he walks in and closes the door behind him: "You do not look so bad yourself in the morning." Albert could not help himself and joins in: "What about me, darling? How do I look?"

Taking a quick glance at Albert, Danny admitted to himself he looked, 'vivid' would be a possible description, so he shared that with Albert: "You look radiant, Albert, as always. A fresh breath of summer."

"I know," is all that Albert said and then added: "Are we ready to go now? Before Danny could answer, his phone rings and Gertie was on the phone. "He is now on his way to breakfast, hurry. Send Toni and Albert down," and Gertie hangs up.

"OK, that was Gertie. You are on. Remember, make an entrance. You left the watch on the nightstand?"

"Of course I have," Albert said pointing towards the nightstand and added: "Sweetness, you do not have to tell me how to be myself," and he grabs Toni's arm, points to the door, which Danny opens and closes behind them.

Danny takes out the tiny black cube from his jacket pocket, the weight of it both insignificant and immense. This was it. Hours of planning culminated in this moment, in this inn room bathed now in the morning orange of a beautiful sun.

The floorboards creaked under his weight as he crept towards the weathered oak nightstand tucked beside the bed. He ran a quick eye around the room, a habit ingrained from years of...well, let's just say, unconventional activities. Satisfied, he knelt beside the nightstand.

The camera, barely bigger than a die, felt cold against his fingers. It had night vision, perfect for the likely scenario of the target in case he entered the room after dark. Danny did not think that was going to happen, but just in case, he made sure his camera purchase night vision.

He needed the placement to be strategic. Too low, and it might get bumped or snagged on drawer contents. Too high, and it wouldn't capture the action.

Brimming with gratitude, Danny appreciated the thoughtfulness of Gertie and Samuel, who strived to make each room unique while understanding the necessity of purchasing certain furniture in bulk for cost efficiency. His gaze darted around the nightstand, and it was identical to the one in his room. There were a few decorative carvings along the top trim. With nimble fingers, he unscrewed a small, innocuous-looking wooden rosette. Behind it, a hollow space gaped, just large enough for the camera. Identical to the one in his room in which he tested the camera.

A surge of satisfaction shot through him.

Perfect, all set.

He wedged the camera into the cavity, adjusting the tiny lens until it had a clear view of the drawer's interior. Danny tested the camera, and the picture was sparkling clear. Taking a deep breath, he carefully screwed the rosette back in place, the wood disguising his handiwork flawlessly. A quick look around confirmed it looked completely natural.

He stood, wiping a small bead of sweat from his brow.

Mission accomplished.

He looked at his watch and by now Toni and Albert had met Abe and should be doing their spiel. Fingers crossed; it all would go as planned.

Danny sat down in a chair and waited.

His mobile rang and Danny listen, and he hangs up and goes towards the door, opens it and as he steps outside, takes one more final look, and closes the door behind him.

Now, all they had to do was wait and hope the camera captured what he needed.

Chapter Forty-Six – Special Friendship

Abe wondered by Gertie had again gone over his departure schedule tomorrow since he had already told her all the details. *"I guess the old girl was just starting to lose some memory,"* he thought, but he did not mind and after he concluded repeating everything to her, he headed towards the dining area. As he enters the dining room Samuel grabs his attention: "Mr Reynolds, good morning. You are a little late. What happen? You are usually at the door at 8 AM sharp to have your breakfast."

"Well, it seems that this morning your lovely spouse Gertie asked me to confirm my departure schedule. It seems she lost her notes and just did not want to relay on her memory. No biggie, just a few minutes. I am sure breakfast will be as delicious as it is always. Yes?"

"Of course it will be Mr Reynolds," Samuel said, and he notices Albert and Toni walking in and aloud says: "Hi Toni, Mr Guzman, good morning. Ready for breakfast?"

"Yes Samuel. Danny is running a little late, so we can sit down wherever you want us to."

"Mr Reynolds, you met Mr Guzman?"

"Yes, I have and of course I know Toni."

"Would it be OK if they shared this table with you today and when Mr Monk comes down, maybe he can join you?"

"That would be wonderful, of course. Please sit."

"Such a charming gentleman," Albert said, extending his left hand in a handshake which Reynolds took.

"Oh, you are not wearing that magnificent TAG Heuer Carrera watch today? You may have heard my own watch was pinched recently."

"Abe darling, yes, I heard that. Terrible, just terrible, but my TAG watch would not do today for my darling friend and his sweetheart," pointing and smiling at Toni, "Toni and Danny are taking me on an ocean voyage and this watch goes much better with my outfit. I am leaving my grandfather's watch in my room, safe and dry. What do you think of this watch, Abe?"

"Well, yes, dry, that is for sure and this watch," pointing to the Seiko, "is a fine watch, but not as expensive, I suppose."

"You are, darling. It is one of those inexpensive watches from Seiko, but I like the colour of its case: black and gold, a yellowish gold, which matches the streaks of my shoes. You like?"

Toni jumped into the conversation. "Albert, that is an eight-hundred dollars watch from Seiko. I would not say it is an inexpensive watch, dear. Some folks would love to have one, I am sure."

"I am sure they would," and with that Albert gave Reynolds a quick verbal dissertation of the ocean trip Danny was taking him today and the times of departure and arrival.

"Well, it sounds like you will have a busy day and look who just walked in the door?" stated Abe as he looks at Danny.

"Good morning, everyone. May I join you for breakfast I am starved?"

"Of course," Abe answered. "I hear you are taking Albert and your sweetheart on an ocean voyage today."

Danny was ready for anything this morning, but Abe calling Toni his sweetheart took him aback a bit and he was lost for words.

"My, oh, my Daniel Monk, lost for words this morning," said Toni with a smile on her face.

Danny stammered, cheeks flushing a faint pink, "Sweetheart? I, uh... I thought you were just... you know, special friends."

Toni's smile widened, a playful glint in her eyes. "Is that all you thought we were, Danny? Special friends?"

"Oh goodness, I started trouble in paradise. I do apologise," stated Abe.

Toni grabs Abe's hand and just says: "Not to worry, Abe. I am sure Danny, and I will have a conversation about our 'friendship' today on, what did Albert call it, our ocean voyage?"

"And I will be there as a witness. I love it. Let us order breakfast," and with that, they each picked up their menu. Toni waved Robert over, who took their order and marched off to the kitchen.

More guests started coming in each n their own little world as they sat down, giving Abe a look or two.

"Abe cariño, why is everyone looking at you so strangely?" asked Albert.

"It seems everyone is a bit mad at me because my watch was stolen, and it is possible they feel I might have insinuated it was a guest that stole it."

"Did you say that, Abe?" asked Danny.

"Well, not directly, but I might have given hints to that matter, but you know how people are, right?"

"Yes, we do, Abe, yes we do," just then Robert returned with all their breakfast plates and the conversation changed to the enjoyment of the meal.

After a few bites Albert leads over to Abe and asks: "Why don't you come with us, Abe? I am sure we would love your company."

"Oh crap," thought Danny, that was not the plan. What was Albert up to?

"So lovely for you to invite me I would love to, but I am leaving tomorrow and today I thought I just head into Crystal Cove and walk around a bit, maybe buy a book."

"That is a shame, Abe it would have been wonderful, but may I make a suggestion concerning your book purchase?"

"Of course, Albert, please share."

"I highly recommend one of Northport's local authors. His name is J. F. Nodar, and he has published two novels out which are quite interesting. The titles are *Books, Pens & Larceny* and the other one. His new science fiction goes with the title *The Universe Between Us*. They are quite good, I hear."

Danny was shaking his head, well, mentally anyway, and could not help himself and asked: "Albert, did you pick up those books before coming up to Crystal Cove?"

"Eh, no, Danny, I forgot. I am sure I can pick one up when I return."

"There is a lovely bookshop in town called *Crystal Cove Bookshop* I am sure they may have it if their stock is large enough. They are very trendy and carry a lot of local authors as well," added Toni.

"Great. I might just do that."

With that, Abe got up, bid his farewells, and headed upstairs.

The three musketeers stared as he went upstairs and then both Toni and Albert turn to Danny with Albert whispering: "You think he is going into my room now?"

"To answer your question, no, I do not think so. He will wait until the rooms are clean after noon or so, probably early afternoon when he returns from his visit to Crystal Cove and before we return from our trip. Albert, what the hell were you thinking when you asked him to come with us on the trip? What if he accepted? He would have no chance later in the day to grab the watch. You could have ruined everything."

"My darling boy. You obviously do not know how to read people. Did you notice how his lip twitched a little on his left side when I made that suggestion?"

Both Toni and Danny looked at each other and simultaneous answered: "No."

"I did and I read that to be he lied about even considering coming with us on the ocean voyage."

"Albert, a twitching lip on its own is not a reliable indicator of lying. It could be anything," said Toni.

"I am right Toni; I know I am right. He sounded so good, like was really thinking of coming, but he has plans. When I mentioned I was leaving my grandfather's watch on the nightstand, I swear there was a sparkle in his eyes. I think your plan, Danny, is going to work. He has taken the bait."

Samuel walks up to them with a couple of plates in his hands and leans over to Danny: "How did it go? Did he take the bait?"

"Yes, I believe he has. We now just wait for him to act."

"Great," said Samuel, "you call me when you feel I need to contact the detective. He said he can be here in ten minutes."

"Good, because while we will be on a boat, we will not be far in the ocean."

"What? Why did I get so dressed up for if I am not going on an ocean voyage?" adds Albert.

"Because Albert, your watch was the bread of the sandwich we presented to Abe, but you, my friend, you are the ham."

"I am not sure I can take that as a compliment, Danny?"

Toni laughs and looks at Danny and says: "Now, let get ready to go and," looking at Danny, "you and I need to have a conversation about our 'special friendship' you mentioned to Abe."

Chapter Forty-Seven – Captain Cora

Albert hurry upstairs to make sure his watch was still there while Danny and Toni moved up the stairs in a solemn walk. Both were quiet, each in their own thoughts. They saw albert wave to them as he walked into his room, and he said: "Thirty minutes by your car Danny?" to which Danny just nodded.

Opening his own door, Danny allowed Toni to walk in first and closed the door behind him and as he turned to face Toni, she just said one word: "Explain."

Danny motioned to Toni towards the lounge, and they sat down.

His eyes fixed on hers, his heart pounding with a mix of nervousness and excitement. Danny took a deep breath, ready to pour out his feelings for her with no hesitation.

"Toni," he began, his voice steady yet filled with emotion, "from the moment I met you, I knew there was something special about you. It wasn't just your beauty or your charm, though those are undeniable. It was something deeper, something that drew me to you like a magnet."

He paused, searching for the right words to express the depth of his feelings. "I love the way you laugh, how it lights up the room and makes everything seem brighter. I love the way you care for others, always putting their needs before your own. And I love the way you challenge me and make me laugh."

Danny reached for her hand. "But most of all, I love the way you make me feel. When I'm with you, I feel like I can be completely myself, like I don't have to pretend to be anyone else. You accept me for who I am, flaws and all, and that's a rare gift."

Toni's eyes shimmered with unshed tears as she squeezed Danny's hand in return. "Danny," she whispered, her voice barely loud to be heard, "I feel the same way about you. You make me happier than I ever thought possible, and I can't imagine my life without you in it."

As they sat there, hand in hand, for a few moments, Toni broke the silence with: "Are you going to kiss me or what Daniel Monk?"

Danny took her face in the cup of his hands and gave Toni what she felt was the sweetest kiss she had ever had.

Toni sighed as Danny released her and Danny smile and prompted her with a "Let's go get ourselves a thief." and took her hand to help her get up and they both march out of the room and headed outside where they saw Albert waiting by Danny's car.

"Samuel pointed out Abe's car to me and it is not now in the parking area. Wait one second. Oh, my goodness, there is a glow, a corona, an aura above you both. Tell me you made up and got this silly 'special friendship' all sorted out."

"We have Albert," said Toni, "we no longer have a 'special relationship' we are now in a committed relationship, right, honey."

A big smiling Danny just said: "Right."

"What time are we expected at the harbour?" Toni asked.

"No specific time. I booked a charter for all day from 9AM until whatever time we need it. The captain was very amicable, especially when the price quoted was not an issue and I gave my AMEX credit card number and it magically showed up as 'approved' on the screen. We will find one happy captain when we arrive at the harbour."

"OK, then darlings, let's go and Toni, I want all the gossip girlfriend. Tell me everything Danny said to you."

As they drove to the harbour, Toni relegated Danny's conversation and her simple response and albert could not help himself and needed to take out a handkerchief for his sniffles.

"You two are making me cry all the time. It is wonderful to have tears of joy."

Arriving at the harbour, Danny parked and said: OK, let's go find the Song Seeker. That is the name of the whale watching boat I hire for us. The captain's name is Cora Marietta. She has five crew members on the boat, and it should be an interesting cruise.

In no time, the Song Seeker was found, and Danny yelled: "Ahoy Captain Cora, permission to come aboard!"

He heard a loud laughter coming from the bow of the boat: "Is that you, Mr Monk? I was expecting you, not Errol Flynn calling me. Welcome to you and your party. Come on board. We are ready when you say the word."

Boarding the boat, albert was a bit wobbly and almost stumble, but a huge pair of hands grabbed his arm and looking up he saw an adonis of a young man.

"Oh, my goodness, you saved me! Thank you so much....," hinting to get a name.

With a big grin, the young Adonis answered: "Bruce, Bruce Laramie, I am Captain's Cora first mate, at your service," and he went about getting ready to shove off.

Albert grins, looks at Toni and in a naughty manner said: "He can be serving me anytime."

"Oh, Albert, stop it. He could be your grandson!"

With a look of insult all Albert said back to Toni was: "I thought you were my friend but with that statement, I am beginning to wonder," and he went toward the stern of the boat where there were deck chairs setup.

Toni finds Danny on the starboard side of the boat, checking his phone. "What are you doing, honey?"

Turning towards Toni he thinks to himself: "I like how she calls me honey," and quickly answers her. "I am making sure I have reception of the camera and it looks great. Here look."

Toni glances and sees one of the house cleaners doing Albert's room. "That's Becky. Goodness, the clarify of the camera is superb. This should work, Danny. We just need Abe to act soon."

"He will. The bait is too much, and I have a good idea what really happens to his watch is going to net him a large insurance claim, at no cost to him, by the way."

Toni was going to say something, but Captain Cora interrupted: "Mr Monk, are we shoving off or not? The ocean is calling us. I can feel it."

"Yes, let's shove off, but you know the drill, Captain, not too far from the harbour. We need a quick return at a moment's notice."

"I do, sir. It is your money, after all, and my father always said the customer is almost right every time."

"Almost every time? Is it not the customer is right always."

"Not in his book."

And with that, Captain Cora waves her right hand above her head and the Song Seeker casts off.

Chapter Forty-Eight – Second Watch

From his advantage point, Abe has been watching the harbour for over thirty minutes, waiting for Monk and his friends to arrive and since he has always been a patient man, he was rewarded when the red convertible showed up and the three occupants got out.

One of the few hobbies Abe has enjoyed over the years was bird watching. He enjoyed entering country fields and the large national parks to do this activity. For this reason, he always had his binoculars in the boot of his car because he would often stop on a drive and do some spotting. Today, those binoculars presented a good closeup of the three breakfast companions.

"That pompous old fart was telling the truth. His friends are taking him on a sea voyage," Abe thought to himself. A sea voyage, as Albert called it, turned out to be just a whale watching excursion. The outcome of this exercise during this time of the year remains uncertain, as there is an equal chance of it being successful or unsuccessful, whether it involves spotting a pod of whales or just one whale. Abe did not care about that. He just wanted to be sure that these three were out of his hair for at least three hours today. Abe also did a bit of research on his phone while waiting and found that the three whale watching vessels in the harbour catered to different economic circles, so he concentrated on the lower to middle upper range price when scanning the harbour.

One boat was way too big, but the second one, the Song Seeker, would do the trick for this trio today. Being the smaller one, it seemed to cater to family events and small corporate group outings since its capacity was only twenty individuals and at $129 dollars for a three-hour whale watching trip per person. It brings in a tidy sum.

Today, thought the Song seeker only had three passengers. Abe did the math in his head and thought aloud: *"This small outing cost Monk over $7,000. He must have a very profitable bookstore. I may have to visit his little town, Northport, and check the place out."*

Abe realises there is movement, and sees the Song Seeker is shoving off, going out of the harbour. A relentless curiosity propelled him forward, pushing him to validate his excuse of visiting the bookstore in case anyone asked. Moreover, the challenge of finding a truly captivating book was becoming increasingly daunting, particularly with the absurd suggestions from Albert.

Abe headed back to his car, took one more look at the harbour and the song Seeker leaving its heads and thought to himself: *"Yes, I am good to go,"* and pointed his car towards the bookstore to browse a bit and give the Song Seeker plenty of time to get into the middle of the ocean before he would go back to the inn and see if he can get himself a second watch out of this holiday trip.

Chapter Forty-Nine – Phone Ping

The three had moved to the stern of the Song Seeker to enjoy the deck chairs provided and Toni could not help but ask. "Danny, how much did this little trip cost?"

Danny thought he should not say how much, but rather respond to the question with a question of his own: "Does it matter, Toni? I have the funds available, and they are just sitting on an account earnings interest. Why not spent it? Enjoy the trip and while we may not go too far offshore there is an off chance, according to Captain Cora, that a whale might swim past us, even this close to shore."

"In other words, you are not answering me, right?"

Danny was going to answer, but Bruce saved the day: "Cocktails, anyone?"

"Oh, Bruce sweetheart, you are a lifesaver. I am roasting out here and a Mojito might just refresh me. Can you make us some?"

"I certainly, sir. I will make a jug of it and bring it out in a few minutes."

"Please darling call, me Alberto. We are here in this vast ocean, and we need to have friends, do we not, yes?"

Bruce smiled back at Albert but did not answer, just saying: "I will be right back with your drinks."

When Bruce goes inside to make the drinks, Danny asks: "Albert, since when you go by Alberto?"

Albert leans forward from his chair and just says: "Danny, have you taken a good look at Bruce? He is beautiful and a beautiful man needs a friend with an exotic first name. Albert will not do on this cruise."

Turning to Toni, Albert asks her: "He is beautiful right dear?"

"He is not my type, Albert. I like them short, fat, and ugly."

"Hey, you are not referring to me? Right?" snaps an unhappy Danny.

"Yes honey, I am. Short, fat and ugly, just like I like them and hence you."

"Well, I will have to take you to an optometrist as soon as we reach shore to have those pretty eyes of yours checked for. I believe they need adjusting."

They all laughed together as Bruce brought the drinks and after pouring them, Albert asks again: "Anything? Anything going on in my room, Danny? Where is Abe anyway? We only have so much time before we go back to shore, right?"

Taking out his phone and showing it to Albert, Danny answers him: "No Albert, look, you do not see a ping indicating entry to your room since Becky tidy it up for you this morning. I will get a ping and then we can watch, so relax. It will happen when it happens."

"The suspense is killing me as well, Danny," added Toni.

"I am not speaking to you."

Again, this brought laughter, for Danny's tone was just playful in his response.

Another hour had passed, and Captain Cora shows up with a great proposal: "Lady and gentlemen, would you like something to eat? Our cook is not a five-star chef but has wiped up an excellent lunch for you. He has prepared as an entrée jumbo prawns marinated in a mixture of coconut milk, lime juice, garlic and ginger. They are skewered and grilled to perfection, imparting a smoky flavour and they are served with a side of tangy mango salsa for a burst of tropical freshness. Then as a main he has come up with fresh Mahi-Mahi fillets seasoned with a blend of spices like paprika, cumin and coriander, pan-seared until golden-brown and crispy on the outside, while remaining tender and flaky on the inside. The fish come with a vibrant pineapple salsa made with diced pineapple, red onion, jalapeño, cilantro and lime juice, adding a sweet and spicy contrast to the fish and it is accompanied by a side of coconut rice and grilled asparagus to complement the flavours. Hoping this has not filled you up, he has made a dessert that is to kill for. It is a creamy and luscious panna cotta infused with coconut milk and fresh mango puree. You folks are ready?"

The three musketeers looked at each other and Albert had to ask: "Any wine?"

"Of course, I will have Bruce bring out a bottle of Sauvignon Blanc from New Zealand, which will just top the meal for you. Does that meet your approval, Mr Monk?"

Impressed, Danny just answered with a simple nod and a raising of his Mojito glass, which Captain Cora returned with a small bow and headed inside to tell Bruce of the wine order and have the chef bring the food out.

"Was that part of the cost of the boat?" asked Toni, wondering how much that meal would cost.

"Not sure, honey. Will know at the end of the trip. Let's enjoy the food and not worry about that."

"Hear, hear," said Albert, getting up and grabbing the Mojito jug and pour all more drink.

Twenty minutes later, Bruce announced that lunch was ready in the mess hall, and they went in.

Walking into the mess hall, Albert gasp: "This is spectacular. It even has a chandelier! Why in the world did Bruce call it a mess, anyway?"

"Albert historically, the term mess originally referred to a group of people who ate together, often in a communal setting. This term was commonly used in military contexts, where soldiers or sailors would gather to eat together. Over time, this term evolved to also refer to the physical location where such communal meals were served," answered Toni.

Looking at Toni, Danny added: "My, oh my, are we a know it all? When did you learn that bit of information, Toni?"

Placing her glass on the table Toni gestures to the windows where you can see the vast ocean simmering in its blue hues: "Look where I lived for many years, Danny. Something must rub off."

Again, they laughed at her answer and sat down just as the chef arrived with their entrees. After enjoying the jumbo prawns, Bruce takes out the plates and in a few seconds in comes in the chef once again, this time with the fish, which looked just beautiful on their plates. Bruce is kept busy pouring the New

Zealand wine, even with Albert interrupting him, making googly eyes, and batting his eyelashes at him.

Finishing their meal, Danny proclaims: "Now that would make our chef at petite Maison a run for his money."

"Our chef? You own a restaurant?" Toni queried.

"Yes, a few other things as well. We are a diversified venture," a little slurry Albert responds.

"You are going to have to explain more of this, Mr Monk, when we have a moment together."

"Yes dear," said Danny, looking at Toni with nothing but love towards her. He was going to add some sentimental statement when Captain Cora walked in holding three plates with their desserts.

"Ah, I see you are ready for dessert," and carefully placing one plate to the side of the empty fish plates, she gingerly picks the empty plates, turns, and adds: "Be sure you save some room for a little brandy. If you do not mind, I mind join you and let my first mate do the honours of sailing the rest of the time."

"Please do, Captain Cora," said Danny, "I am sure you can relegate some sea stories to us while we enjoy the brandy." Before Captain Cora can respond, Danny receives a loud phone ping. A quick look brings a smile to his face, and he signals Toni and Albert over. When they too do a glance at the phone's screen, that same smile appeared on their faces.

"Captain, we are going to give the brandy a pass. How quickly can you get us back into the harbour and our car?"

"Since you asked me just to get you out of view of shore and then just move back and forth so we would not be far, no more than twenty minutes. Will that do?"

"It will just find Captain. Thank you."

Captain Cora leaves the mess hall and heads toward the bridge, leaving her guests in the mess hall.

"*A strange trio, but then again, everything paid up front and Mr Monk even added a generous trip. I wonder what they are up to in Crystal Cove?*" shrugged the captain as she gave an order for the boat to return to its port.

Chapter Fifty – Roebuck S. Cooke

To his surprise Abe made a purchase in the bookstore. He purchased another book by the same author titled *Mending Hearts in Crystal Cove*, which was a great title and coincidentally shared the same town name. The bookstore clerk it was a crime and romance story, so why not? It had a reasonable price and a beautiful cover. After paying for it, he headed back to the inn and going past reception he made a point to stop and tell Gertie he had purchased the book and was going to check out in about an hour since something had come up that require his attention back home.

"How about lunch, Mr Reynolds? Will you have lunch here before you leave?"

"No Gertie. No time. I will grab something on the way home. Please have the bill ready so we can settle before I leave," and with that, Abe went up the stairs.

No one expected this. This was not what Danny, and the rest had planned, so she gave Danny a quick ring, but the phone was engaged, so she placed her receiver down and decided to give the telephone line a few minutes before calling back.

Abe wasted no time.

First, he noticed that someone had serviced his room and most likely the rest of the inn's rooms had been taken care of as well. He quickly packed. Did not bother to fold anything and just made sure he took everything from the bathroom that might provide DNA samples. After he packed, he took out several microfiber clothes and cotton cloths he always carried and wipe down every surface he believes he might have touched while staying in the room. Finishing that, he retrieved his lock picking kit and headed into the hall.

No one was in the hall, so Abe moved swiftly towards Albert's room door and quickly opened it. Abe looked for the watch on the nightstand and there it was, just laying there for the taking. "*Was this too easy?*" he thought. His experience was that most people would at least attempt some concealment of their valuables if they do not use a hotel's safe. They will hide the valuable in the bathroom, or in their toiletry bag, inside luggage or their clothing. This looked suspicious to Abe, so he stood there. Not moving for a few minutes, thinking.

Abe looked around the room. Everything seemed in order. Why was he worried? He never worried before. He would enter the room, for the first time with a sleeping drunk in it, take what he wanted. Why the hesitation today?

After a few minutes, Abe relaxed. He had nothing to worry about. The fool probably was rich like Monk and did not worry about things like that. "*Yes, I am sure he does not worry about things like theft occurring to him. Such a pompous, selfish old fart,*" Abe surmised in his mind and with that, Abe grabs the watch and places in his pocket.

Once again, he wipes down the nightstand and the inside doorknob and opens the door. Once again, no one is in the hall, so he closes the door, wipes the outside doorknob and heads to his own room as if nothing had happened.

Gertie finally got in touch with Danny, and they compared notes and after taking Danny's suggestions, she got Samuel to go outside and find Abe's car and deflated one of the rear tyres to delay his departure. As soon as she gave Samuel his marching orders, she rang the detective and told him to hurry to the inn. "It has happened, and he is leaving soon," was all Gertie said to detective Callum.

Looking at the time, it was a few minutes before checking in time and Gertie checked her calendar. *"Good, only one new guest coming in. He said he was not sure of the time but would be in shortly after check in time. Hopefully this all will be over soon,"* she thought.

Gertie sees Samuel coming in and gives her a nod, stating to her that his task of deflating the tyre had been done. *"Good heavens. Where were Danny and the rest?"* Gertie muttered to herself, worry they might be running late, thought Danny said they would be here in an hour or so. She looked at her watch. It had been an hour, so maybe they will be walking in through the front door soon.

Just then, Abe walks down the stairs with his two suitcases in hand.

"Hi Gertie. Do you have my bill ready?"

"Yes, I do. It will only take a moment to print. Would you like Robert to take your suitcases out to your car?"

"No, that will not be necessary I can roll them out. The bill please I want to hit the road before rush hour."

Laughing to make time, Gertie said: "That is funny Mr Reynolds. There is no rush hour in Crystal Cove. Really funny," and Gertie continues fidgeting with the computer.

Abe was starting to get annoyed at the delay but did not want to make a scene and bring attention to himself and, being a patient man, he waited for the bill to print.

"Well, hello there, Abe. Going somewhere?" Abe hears and turns to see Danny, Albert and Toni walking in.

"Hello back Danny. Yes, received a call from home and I need to check out early so I am waiting for my bill so I may pay it and get on the road."

"We never had that coffee, Abe. How about we grab a cuppa and then you leave?"

"Love to, but no time. Anytime soon with the bill, Gertie?" now sounding irritated.

Not able to delay any longer, Gertie hits the print key, and the bill spills out in two seconds and she hands it to Abe, who does a quick perusal, and hands her his VISA card for payment.

"As fast you can, Gertie, I need to go. It is getting late for me. I do not like driving at night and the longer I must wait, the more the possibility I will not reach home before dark."

Gertie does the credit card processing and Abe signs it, waits for his receipt and turns to Danny and the rest.

"It has been a pleasure. Hoping your stay will be as nice as it has been for me," bye for now.

Abe grabs his two suitcases and starts rolling them out the door and they close behind him.

Danny turns and looks at Gertie: "Are we good?"

With a smile on her face, Gertie just says: "Samuel did his part."

"Good. Now let's go into the dining room and wait for Abe to return."

Walking in, they see that the dining room has some guests having afternoon tea. Mr Aloysius and Mrs Evelyn Maxwell are there having tea while the honeymooners, Jim and Sally Wentworth, seem to be enjoying cocktails instead of the usual coffee or tea. Finally, Ms Lititz Carter, as always all decked out to the nines, is wetting her lips with a Mimosa. The only one missing was Mr Homer Witham, who had checkout this morning.

Samuel walks up to them and whispers: "You heard?"

"Yes, we have Samuel. Thanks for doing that. How about some coffee when you have a moment?"

"I will have Robert take your orders. I want to see what happens when Reynolds finds the flat tyre. Keep you posted."

Samuel heads back towards the bar and speaks to Robert, who walks over to take our coffee orders while Samuel goes into the kitchen.

After Robert takes out the order, Albert cannot contain himself: "What now Danny? What if Abe sees the flat tyre and simply just fixes it himself? He will leave, and I do not see that young detective anywhere. Do you?"

"Albert. I have watched Abe Reynolds. He is not going to do his own tyre fixing. He either will have some road service company in his car, or he will ask for help. He is not the type to do much of physical work these days. In his youth maybe, but not now."

As if by summon Abe walks into the dining room.

"It seems I am destined not to leave early. I have a flat tyre. Since I have no road service with my car, I asked Gertie for help. She said to wait here, have a coffee and she will handle it for me. So, you mind if I join you for that cuppa we spoked about early?"

"By all means, Abe, please sit," and Danny waves to Robert to come over and take Abe's order—an expresso.

A minute or two later, Robert walks back with Abe's coffee.

The table is silence and Abe feels the tension and asks: "Is everything all right? All of you seem a bit tense. Something happen on your boat trip?"

Before Danny could speak, Gertie pops her head in the dining room and gives shim a thumbs up.

"*OK*," thought Danny, "*here we go.*"

"Yes, Abe, as a matter of fact, something did happen while we were on the boat. There was a robbery."

"Oh, my goodness. Did someone on the boat steal from one of you, or maybe from your car? What happen? Tell me."

"I can do better than that, Abe. I can show you," and Danny takes his phone out and punches a few buttons.

"Tell me what you see, Abe," was all Danny said.

Danny hands Abe his phone, and Abe starts watching the video of himself as he stands in Albert's room. He watches himself doing what he did during his entry. He hands Danny back the phone back and does not say anything.

Abe then starts laughing. So loudly that all the guests turn to look at him.

"That video means nothing. I am leaving," and Abe gets up, but as he nears the door, detective Liam Callum and two New South Wales police officers block his path.

"Mr Reynolds, please place your hands behind your back. You are under arrested for the attempted theft of Mr Guzman's watch and the possible defraud attempt of your insurance company."

"You have nothing. No proof. Just a deep fake video."

With that, a third office shows up with one of Abe's suitcases and opens it to reveal Albert's watch and the supposedly stolen watch that Abe reported alone with the written report that Abe signed to claim his insurance.

Abe did not say anything else, and Detective Cullum hands him to the two police officers that lead him towards the front door as the detective, Danny, Albert, Toni, Samuel and Gertie following like in a conga line to watch Abe walk out the door to see a tow truck loading his car up and three other police vehicles waiting next to Abe's car.

Danny notices a BMW X4 sport drive up and park with a middle-aged man getting out, watching all that is going on.

"Goodness, when do you think I will see my watch, detective?" shyly asks Albert.

"We will need to keep it as evidence for a while, but it should not be long. Thank you all for helping out with this case," and he brings out an enormous smile and looks at Danny: "I will have to tell senior detective Cassell of your help."

"Yes, you do that," answered Danny almost sarcastically, making Cullum laugh aloud as he steps out the front door.

The group head towards the reception counter and both Samuel and Gertie go behind it while Danny, Albert and Toni face them. Toni giggles a bit and says: "That was not expected. Danny Monk, you brought excitement to Crystal Cove with your stay here."

"I did not mean to. I came to mend, and I did that by finding you, Toni. Catching Abe was a plus."

"Hear, hear," said Albert, "let's go to the bar and grab some drinks they are all on Danny's tab," and he turns and bumps into the middle-aged man from the car.

Albert looks at the man and reacts: "My, you are a tall one and handsome, to boot. Glad I bump into you. I will be at the bar with my friends if you care to join us. My name is Albert Matthew Guzman and my friend Danny Monk and his girl, Toni Webster. And you are?" Albert, smiling, asks.

"My name is Roebuck S. Cooke."

"Yes, Mr Cooke," interjects Gertie, "welcome, we have been expecting you're your room is ready. You will be staying in the Lighthouse Loft. Your room is ready. Do you need help with your luggage?"

"No, I am fine. Can you tell me what happen here?"

"Oh, darling, that little man stole my watch, and we caught him. The police just took him away as you saw," interjected Albert.

"You helped catch him. All of you?"

"Yes darling. We did. We are practically police officers."

"Mr Cooke, please do not listen to my friend, he tends to over blow a situation. Yes, we helped, but we are not police officers. Just concerned citizens."

"Good to know that there are still good people in the world. I do not see many in my kind of work."

"Darling, what do you do for a living?" again inquired albert.

"I own a private detective agency, Adler and Finch Investigations," and he hands out his card.

"And you are here in Crystal Cove for...," asks Toni.

"A much-needed rest. I just closed my office in the Sydney CBD after a successful case involving larceny and recovery of stolen art objects and antiques. Did so well that I will be hiring some associates to help me grow the business. I plan to specialise in this type of work in the future, contracting for insurance companies on a recovery percentage basis on their old cold cases. So, with the funds I earned, I decided to leave the CBD, and head to the suburbs and found a well-to-do town. I just purchased a building, and I am waiting for the contractor to finish the remodelling the architect designed to the office space and for new furniture to arrive. You might have heard of it of the small town. It is called Northport."

Danny and Albert look at each other and then at Toni.

Albert's mouth opens and all you hear is him say: "Oh crap."

About the Author

José F. Nodar

Flung into one of life's biggest challenges at just eleven, José's story began in Havana, Cuba. The Cuban revolution forced him onto a plane alone, landing him at an orphanage in a small Georgia town called Washington. Reuniting with his parents wouldn't happen until he was eighteen, a high school graduate in Atlanta.

Business Administration became his focus at Georgia State University. From there, he navigated the world of finance, first at the First National Bank of Atlanta (now Wells Fargo) and later as a project manager in financial consulting. These roles took him across the United States, Europe, and even Australia.

It was in Camden, New South Wales, Australia, that a spark ignited José's creative side. A writers' group became the launching pad for his debut novel, and soon, his mind birthed Danny Monk, his first major character.

Currently, José is a prolific writer, working on his seventh short story collection alongside a new crime novel slated for release in 2026.

But José's life isn't all about writing. When he's not crafting captivating stories, you might find him at the local mall, observing the world and gathering inspiration for future characters. Away from his computer, he dives into books or enjoys long, leisurely walks with his wife Miriam around Camden.